The Storm

By: Marian Gardner

Thank You Sherri
The memories of you
will always be special
May the rest of your life
continue with many years
of love and happiness

Foreve Friend

Marian Gardner

Table of Contents

Dedication……………………………………………………Page 5

Authors Note……………………………………………….Page 6

Foreword…………………………………………………….Page 8

Chapter One: The Arrangement…………………………Page 10

Chapter Two: Kangaroo Island……………………….Page 19

Chapter Three: Flashback………………………………Page 29

Chapter Four: The Children……………………………Page 39

Chapter Five: The Employees…………………………Page 49

Chapter Six: Commanding the Room………………Page 59

Chapter Seven: Focused & Driven…………………Page 67

Chapter Eight: The Wedding…………………………Page 79

Chapter Nine: The Biggest Merger…………………Page 92

Chapter Ten: He Shall Live and Not Die……………Page 104

Chapter Eleven: The Miracle…………………………Page 117

Chapter Twelve: Ann, A Pillar of Strength…………Page 135

Chapter Thirteen: Too Old to Have a Baby…………Page 151

Chapter Fourteen: Paradise Restored....................Page 162

Chapter Fifteen: Tragedy Strikes...........................Page 178

Chapter Sixteen: Tragedy Strikes Twice................Page 193

Chapter Fifteen: Epilogue.....................................Page 210

Dedication

I dedicate this book to those I love who have endured the suffering and pain of this life. By His Grace you will make it through.

To my husband James who knows my labor of love

To my adult children, Tammey, Stephanie and Maurice,
Love always,
Mother.

God's second greatest gift is who he chose to be our parents. Lord, I thank you for John and Lurleen Cameron.
I thank you for putting me in a Godly home, where my mother exposed me to Jesus at an early age.

Author's Note

I have always had a desire to write fiction and Christian books. I allowed my lack of education, self-worth and numerous excuses to keep me from trying. I attended Bethany Bible College and excelled in my studies, graduating in 2003. My son Maurice said I was able to excel because I loved the Word of God. My best friend and cousin, Lou Verne Brickey was my biggest cheerleader. She always enjoyed reading my short stories. She always told me that I can pay people to correct my punctuation and grammar. She would be proud to know I finally did what she said I could do.

Being led by the voice of the God of my salvation, I left Ohio. I have never had to look back. My mother said, Marian God was in Ohio, you didn't have to go to California to find Him. I arrived in Pasadena, California in January 1983, and have been in the ministry here for the past 38 years. I have fostered 19 children in my home for the last 15 years and have seen souls brought into the kingdom of God.

I have made mistakes and Jesus who saved me by his blood has taught me that I'm not able to do it without Him. Prayer does not fix everyone and everything the way we want it to be fixed, but it helps to know that God answers by His Grace and Mercy.

My desire is for my book, The Tropical Storm, is that it will open the minds of hurting people that are struggling with pain and disappointments. My prayer is that they will become overcomers. No amount money can replace the peace of God. The characters in my book had money, but they all learned that money could not buy peace and contentment.

I want to thank my Pastor Gary B. Parks and LOV Fellowship Center for their love and support

Foreword

God rebuked the idea that the Gospel should be confined inside of the four walls of a building. His desire has always been for His disciples go into the highways and byways to save the lost. This book makes the Word of God more accessible to those who enjoy reading fiction.

The Gospel comes alive through the trials, tribulations and everyday characters in this book, as they walk out their lives. The struggles and questions asked by the characters in this book are common to all of us. Wrestling gives us the opportunity to come to grips with reality and to make sense of those things in life that we don't understand.

It is refreshing to know that we all have access to the Creator, no matter how much we struggle. It is even better to know that God's grace and mercy is extended to all of us, even those who consider themselves Atheists. We were meant to be searchers of truth. Without questioning, we can never find answers to that which we don't understand. God's desire is that we all come to know the truth.

From childhood trauma, marital problems, infidelity, and alcoholism, the situations and scenarios in this book are ones in which we can all identify. The character of Abigail helps the reader understand how childhood trauma can create a lasting impact, well into adulthood. Addison is a perfect example of how hurting people hurt people. His story teaches the reader that true fulfillment can't be found in a bottle, or in the attainment of money and power. Ann's story shows the reader that even the best and well thought out plans that we might have for our lives, may not always turnout as planned. Neil demonstrates the guilt and inner struggle that many people face, and the challenges that people endure even after making a decision to change.

This book is a true representation of what I believe Jesus had in mind, when He tells us to follow Him and he would make us fishers of men (Matthew 4:19). We are the only book that some people will read, but others may choose to read fiction, and when they do, it is my hope that if this is the book that they choose, that they might also find salvation.

Dr. Vanessa Enoch

Chapter One: The Arrangement

The storm was forecasted to hit the Eastern Coast of South Carolina early on Tuesday morning, and a mandatory evacuation had been ordered for Columbia, SC. and surrounding cities. In situations like these, you always have your doubters who believe it's not going to be as bad as forecasted, and decide to ride out the storm. Addison Chandler and his family left Columbia a year ago, when a horrific storm was predicted to hit the Columbia Coast, but the hurricane turned back out to the sea before making landfall. Addison decided to take his chances and stay put. He thought this was nothing but another overzealous weather reporter trying to boost his ratings. He mused at how forecasters tended to get people hyped for disasters that usually never happened.

Addison sipped the Remy Martin as it slid smoothly down his throat. He laughed, thinking about how gullible these poor, misguided people are, getting all excited and running out spending money they don't have, and stocking up on supplies they don't need, and worrying about a storm that will probably never come. These naive fools will hear from family and friends they haven't heard from in years, to warn them about a hurricane headed towards them and to check to see if they are okay. Once the hurricane passes, they won't hear from their family till the next unlikely disaster. If the hurricane hit then they would finally have the weather to talk about.

Addison thought things like this was hilarious. He could feel the Remy Martin beginning to take effect. He felt free, like he was on top of the world and nothing and no one and could touch him. He paused for a moment. Then another moment passed, as he began to sink into a stupor. He wished the world would stop and let him off; his head was spinning and nothing was making sense now. How many times had he broken his promise to himself? He truly did not want a drink.

Addison looked down at his hand, wondering how the keys to the liquor cabinet got there. After he'd had a few drinks, he always wondered how they got there. He once threatened his personal secretary with termination and no severance pay if he was able to find the key. He reflected on several conversations he'd had with her when he was completely drunk and out of his mind. On several occasions he had called, a locksmith to rekey the cabinet, "How could this happen again?"

The sound of the fierce winds slamming against the titanium shutters aroused him from his drunken stupor. He knew the hurricane had to be a Category 5 storm, with wind speeds of at least 137 knots. He knew his building could withstand wind speeds of 100 mph, and after that, the building enclosed itself with protective titanium shutters.

Addison consumed the entire bottle of Cognac. He wasn't concerned about his family. He knew wherever they were, they were safe with his wife Abigail. She had probably taken the children and flown to some far away state, where they weren't surrounded by water. He knew he was a selfish bastard, but he hadn't always been that way. He used to be loving, caring, understanding and compassionate. His wealth had given him the privilege to help others who were less fortunate. Addison was always taught to give back, and to not to think of himself more highly than others. He knew he should not think he was better than others. He had been given much, so much was required of him. So, how did he lose his love for people?

Her name was Abigail Elizabeth Stein, the daughter of Jacob and Joanna Stein of New York. She was from one of the wealthiest families in the United States.

How could Addison forget the day he met Abigail? She was smart, confident and beautiful, but she was also conceited, self-centered, and most of all egocentric. She was adored and pampered as a child and she thought she was invincible. She wanted Addison to know that she was superior to him. He read Abigail's mind and quickly realized she would never be his; there were not enough zeros in his bank account. The Stein's wealth was enormous. Addison was intimidated by Abigail's beauty, her posture, her attitude and her wealth. Abigail was determined not to give him the time of day; her parents loved him, but she could care less about pleasing them.

Abigail was five years old when she was kidnapped from her parent's home. The police convinced the Stein's not to pay the ransom, because if word gotten out that they paid a ransom, it would be a never ending nightmare for their family. The trauma of the kidnapping was too much for five year old Abigail. She was damaged emotionally and psychologically. The doctors told her parents that the extent of the trauma was so severe that she might never make a full recovery.

After many years of therapy, Abigail fell in love with James White. She was twenty-five, and had learned to trust again. Her father said James was from the wrong side of the tracks, and he forbade her from seeing him. Abigail pleaded with her father to allow her to see James, but her father knew James could never fit into Abigail's world. Her father sent her away to get over James and she vowed to break every suitor's heart from that day forward.

Her father introduced her to Addison Chandler as his business partner, but Abigail suspected he was grooming him to be her husband. She was determined to intentionally make Addison fall in love with her so that she could break his heart.

Abigail was Jacob's prized possession, and the whole state of New York knew it. Jacob's annual Black and White Ball attracted celebrities and business tycoons from around the world . The whisper in prominent circles around town was that his sole purpose for the ball was to make an exhibition of his daughter's beauty. Potential suitors, especially Addison, would quarrel over their seating arrangements. They would make extravagant and ridiculous business deals to be invited to sit at Jacob's table to be near his daughter.

They bribed one another with stocks, bonds and money; this would go on for several months leading up to the ball, but Abigail paid none of her father's associates any attention. She was rude and arrogant to everyone her father introduced her to. Jacob thought by inviting Addison to his home that he might win the favor of his headstrong daughter. Coming to Jacob's home was on the pretense of discussing the opportunity for Jacob to invest in Addison's brokerage firm, which was the most successful brokerage firm in the country. Addison hired only the top consultants and financial experts. Chandler's Brokerage Firm was nationwide. He was an expert at buying, selling and trading stocks.

Addison had an appointment to meet with Jacob at his home, but instead of the butler taking him to his office, he was instructed to take him to the dining room. To Addison's surprise, Abigail was sitting at the dining table when he arrived. As he approached her to speak, she looked straight past him, as though he weren't there and got up from her chair and left the room. Had this encounter been a trap set for him by Jacob? Addison felt humiliated and betrayed. Had Abigail been told he was coming to see her? Addison knew Jacob had been trying to play matchmaker to get the two of them together for quite some time, but blind-siding either one of them wasn't the way to do it.

Addison's anger arose within him. He had never experienced this kind of rejection. He was good looking, wealthy and had a charming personality.

At that moment, Addison couldn't feel anything other than hatred for Abigail. Why had she treated him so badly? He was courteous and respectful, and had always gone out of his way to be nice to her.

"Oh! If she wants war, war I'll give her." Addison thought. "She'll pay for her cruelty toward me."

He knew one day he would have the upper hand, and she would pay dearly for her mistake tonight. He would be as cruel and heartless to her as she had been to him tonight. He swore on his mother's grave he would marry Abigail Stein; he'd make her pay for shattering his dreams, rejecting his affection, and making him feel as though he was less than a man. Addison was going to make her suffer, even if it took the rest of his life. As he obsessed over what would one day be his revenge, evil entered his heart and mind.

Chapter Two: Kangaroo Island

Over the course of his interaction at family and business gatherings, Addison somehow managed to fall in love with Abigail. Even though she had never shown any warmth or affection towards him, he had longed for Abigail's affection for two whole years, often making unnecessary trips to New York, under the guise of doing business with her father. She was aware of Addison's affections towards her and his desperate attempts to please her. But Abigail's behavior was extreme even for her. Addison thought it wise to give her space, and he continued to treat her respectfully. On occasion he would flirt or would try to make her laugh. He wondered if she had always rejected his advances because she was in love with someone else.

On New Year's Eve in 1965, Addison came to New York to ask Abigail's father for her hand in marriage. On his occasional visits to New York, he managed to get her to smile and even engaged Abigail in meaningless banter. Strangely, he began to find her rejection a bit charming. Addison wanted to start the New Year off right, by engaging the beautiful daughter of Jacob, the woman he loved. Jacob was delighted that Addison asked for her hand in marriage.

Jacob had encouraged him not to take Abigail's insults personally. He knew they would be an exceptionally powerful couple, despite the fact that Abigail was headstrong. Jacob knew Abigail needed a powerful man like Addison. He would be firm, yet gentle with his daughter, and he'd still give his princess all that her heart desired.

Abigail was a dream-killer. Once she'd made up her mind that she was going to destroy a man's ego, it was only a matter of time until she had him captivated by her gaze and crying for mercy and deliverance from the utter destruction of his masculinity. Abigail understood what it took to truly damage the male ego beyond repair. She took pleasure shattering Men's dreams. Addison had determined that he wouldn't fall victim, yet with every passing day he felt himself slipping under her spell.

Jacob desired a husband for Abigail who could handle his daughter's stubborn ways, and who could help to manage her finances and wealth once he was no longer around to protect her. She needed an intelligent businessman like Addison. Jacob's only request was that Addison promise to be respectable and good to his daughter? Jacob wanted to know that Abigail would always be treated like the china doll he raised her to be. Abigail was fragile and as breakable as an eggshell, her outer exterior was tough and frigid, but her heart was soft and gentle like any daddy's girl born with a silver spoon in her mouth. Addison knew he could not make this promise, because his intent was to treat her as she had treated him and it wouldn't be like a china doll, but a rag doll. She had destroyed Addison even before she became his wife. He had to admit that despite his earlier nonchalance, the sounds of the raging wind was starting to cause him concern.

Addison listened closely as the winds slammed against the shutters. His cynicism reminded him of how his wife was similar to this raging storm. Like the storm she was winning the battle in their marriage. The storm from the ocean was going to win this battle tonight too. The force of the winds and water was slamming the Coast of South Carolina. Addison knew all his wealth couldn't buy the ocean's loyalty or cooperation. Neither his money, strength, nor power was enough to bribe the ocean. He had been able to bribe Senators, Governors, and City Councilman; he even bribed his board members, but there was no negotiating with the ocean's power tonight. The power of the ocean was far greater than he had imagined. The ocean neither kept score nor hid secrets; countless people over the centuries had made their final resting place in its mouth. The ocean bowed to no one. The raging waves and forceful winds kneeled only to its Creator who set its boundaries. The ocean rode across the seas to return year, after year on its own terms.

The liquor was having its effect on his thinking. Had the storm closed down the city? Was his family safe? Because of Addison's lack of support, Abigail had to be responsible for herself and the children. She attempted to contact Addison on his private line, before she and the children left Columbia. She knew her husband was either with one of his escorts or passed out drunk in his office and would pay no attention to the warning sirens. There would be no need for him to take cover, because he was in a state-of-the art building. If he was in his office building, he would be safe from being blown off the 75th floor. The skyscraper had been built in such a way that once the sirens for a storm went off, the building automatically locked itself down, sealing off glass windows. She figured Addison was probably alone in the building except for the 24-hour armed guards, unless the governor had ordered a total evacuation of the city. If that was the case, the guards would not be in danger of losing their jobs, by abandoning their post. The office staff had left earlier due to the weather forecast. Addison was staying put; he and his family had returned two days earlier, before the storm was forecasted; prior to that, they had been in Indonesia. He wasn't ready to stay in a hotel; he could care less if it was the Ritz-Carlton or the Taj Mahal. For him, there was no place home. Addison wanted to be surrounded by his own possessions, surrounded by the aroma of his own scent, and sleeping in his own bed with his Egyptian cotton sheets, home, sweet home nothing to compare.

Addison almost tripped and lost his balance, as he stumbled to the liquor cabinet to get another bottle of Cognac. His family had traveled around the world. He knew traveling with his children would expand their horizons and educate them far greater than reading about these places in books. As he listened to the wind, he was reminded of the horrific storm that took place ten years ago while his family was on vacation in Australia. A cyclone had hit Kangaroo Island. The people on the island had been warned and ordered by authorities to evacuate three days before the storm was forecasted to make landfall. Addison felt he knew more than any meteorologist. He had seen too many storms turn at the last minute and go back out to sea.

Abigail pleaded with Addison to think of the children and evacuate the island as everyone else had done. The domestic help left without their pay, because Addison refused to pay them if they did not stay till he left. They told him their lives were more important than money and that he would be hearing from their attorney regarding their unpaid wages. At some point, there were no boats left to evacuate his family off of the island. At some point, the only possible way they could have vacated the island would have been by helicopter.

Abigail yelled at him for being a narcissistic self-centered conceited bully, who did not consider his wife's concern for their children. It was too late to share his feelings with his wife and children, too late to tell them that he was afraid. How could he have shared with his family his despair and fears that because of his stubbornness that they were going to die? Their death would be by drowning, because of his inflated pride and thinking himself superior. Addison tried calling his pilot, but was unable to convince him to pick up him and his family. The storm was raging, and the pilot refused to endanger his life and the lives of his own family.

Miraculously they survived the Cyclone, but Addison didn't know how. He had no idea about why they were able to survive. The next morning his three year old daughter, Sarah, attempted to tell her father how an angel had come in the middle of night, and carried them to higher ground. Addison listened to his sweet little Sarah shaking his head as she shared her story; he dismissed the story as a child's fairly tale.

Sarah was the closest thing to an angel he knew and the only one who truly loved him. He could literally feel her love, and sensed that she understood his shortcomings. Sarah never looked at her father with anything but love, no matter how many times he had disappointed her or the rest of the family. She understood that her father was in pain. She empathized with her mother and brothers for their disappointment towards her father. They didn't try to disguise their how they felt towards him, especially when he would stay away from home for days or weeks at a time, or come home drunk. Sarah didn't judge her father, she understood he needed help. She would appeal to her father to call her mother and brothers to let them know he was okay. She had been taught by Nancy, her nanny how to pray for her father and she would pray the same prayer over and over again, always asking Jesus to surround her papa with His angels.

Sarah had overheard her mother talking to her grandmother about her father, and how a man is supposed to act if he truly loves his family. Addison and Abigail had been married for over twenty-five years, yet he was still acting as though he was a bachelor instead of a married man with three children. He was his own man and did as he pleased. He answered to no one, not even his family.

Chapter Three: Flashback

Addison couldn't understand why these memories were coming back tonight, especially his daughter's peculiar survival story. Was it because of the storm? He did not believe in God. He had openly declared he was an atheist. He believed people who served God were weak minded people. People who needed to believe in God, a higher power or a supernatural being lacked confidence in themselves or they were deranged.

Addison believed in evolution. It was his religion and money was his God. His children were forbidden to have any association with organized religion. It had been ten years and there was still no answer about how they survived that night on Kangaroo Island. It still puzzled Addison how his three year old daughter, could tell him a story about angels taking them to higher ground. He knew she had seen paintings and some of her nannies had read books to her about angels. He taught his children that painters and authors had their own interpretation of their work. It had been ten years since this phenomenon occurred. His daughter's story was still etched in the back of his mind. He could not rationally explain away why they had not drowned, or how they managed to get to higher ground? The one regret Addison had once they got to South Carolina was firing his helicopter pilot. If nothing else, he understood that his family was in danger of losing their lives because of him, and his last hope was to have the pilot rescue them. Looking back on the incident, he regretted having his pilot black-balled from flying, but he had made sure he would never work for another corporation as a private pilot.

Was the Cognac talking, or was he getting soft in his old age? Could he be starting to care? For the past ten years, Addison had questioned priest, rabbis, spiritual leaders, gurus, Hindu's, teachers, guides, and experts on supernatural occurrences, but no one could explain this phenomenon to his satisfaction.

There was a priest named Father Thomas, from the Church of The Living God in Rome, who told him it was a miracle from God. Addison had asked Father Thomas, why God would save someone who was uncaring and only concerned about saving himself from death? The priest couldn't explain to Addison why God would save an atheist, other than to show him how much he loved him and wanted him to be in the family of God. This was totally irrational to Addison. Father Thomas also reminded him, he wasn't the only one on the island that night whose life was spared; his whole family including their nanny was with him. He had never thought about that before; he was only thinking of himself, and how he had survived. How truly conceited he was to only think of himself!

Father Thomas tried to explain the gospel of Jesus Christ and his relationship to the Father and the Holy Spirit; Addison smiled smugly and said a few curse words under his breath. He had refused to open his stubborn, cold, stony heart to the gospel, however somehow he was drawn to Father Thomas and despite his misgivings, Addison gave a large donation to the Church of The Living God.

To clear his head he thought maybe he needed to leave the Cognac alone tonight and switch to vodka. He was trying to remember if he might have been drinking Cognac the night of the cyclone in Kangaroo Island? He crawled across the floor to the liquor cabinet, struggling to stand on his legs, which felt like jelly. His hands were tightly wrapped around a bottle of Killian Vodka. Some of his board members were always trying to impress him with their expensive liquors from around the world. On one of the selves was a bottle of Henri IV Dudognon Heritage Cognac Grande Champagne valued at $2.3 million. This was the reason his liquor cabinet was always locked and had an alarm in the event it was open when he was out of the room. Even if he went to his private restroom the cabinet locked down until he returned to the room. It was a lucrative game with him and his business partners making a profit from bringing the expensive champagne into the country on their private jets. Big Wig's from countries where alcohol is prohibited and strictly enforced brought some of his best clients, when they visited the United States. They were willing to splurge their riches, not only on alcohol, but the escort service outranked the alcohol. This was a big deal for Addison, because these men called themselves believers in God. He decided that men of faith were nothing but hypocrites; as he had watched for decades as they all fell short in his eyes, always pretending to be something they weren't.

These weren't what Addison considered the actions of true believers, or at least what Addison called a believer. Father Thomas' explanation had come the closest to what Addison believed to be the best understanding of the gospel, yet even he could not explain the incident which took place on Kangaroo Island that the priest considered a miracle.

Father Thomas didn't explain to him that the gospel is solely the work of Jesus Christ, because despite

Addison's admiration for the priest, he would only allow him to go so far. Addison knew nothing of the transformation of God and that no effort on our part can earn us His gift of grace. All Addison could see was the hypocrisy of men and women alike. It was beyond *Addison's ability to conceive the possibility of a God, a God whose name is Jesus and* to believe He created the entire universe.

Abigail continued to call Addison's private number, but there was still no answer. The Chandler building had been built to withstand a missile attack. His office security had more advanced technology than the White House. In fact his office building was on a national security list as a secure location to bring the President. He could hear the storm increasing in intensity as the winds whipped the shutters; again the liquor was taking him back down memory lane to the dreadful night in Kangaroo Island. Why did he keep reliving this nightmare? His life seems to have been counted in storms, rather than years...with one storm after another.

In Addison's mind, he could hear his mother talking about Jesus calming the raging sea. It was a sea alright, the sea of her anger, lies and frustrations that she took out on his back. He hated that he was ever conceived in her womb. She should have aborted him. Who could worship a God that allowed a baby to suffer the way he suffered? Addison asked Father Thomas, "Are you calling my life a gift of grace from Jesus?" Father Thomas had no idea of what he had suffered in this life. Even his family had no idea. No one knew his past and he spent millions of dollars making sure of it.

Addison had been able to purchase a whole new identity and to erase everything associated with his family. He managed to erase his mother and father. The father wasn't hard because Addison never knew him to begin with.

Addison's ancestors came from Ireland & Scotland and his family went back seven generations to the Chandlers, who were great landowners with large Farms. He knew this was the Cognac talking. He never allowed himself to think about his mother, let alone hear her voice in his mind. He hated her more than he could ever hate Abigail. Maybe his mother had been reincarnated in Abigail. For the mere purpose of torturing his soul even more.

Addison didn't fear hell; he had already lived in hell with his mother. He couldn't bring himself to think about why he was alone in an office building and not some place with his family. In his mind, he kept calling for Abigail and Sarah, but they were not answering him. Where were they? Had they gone to get him food? Where were his sons? This time the sirens aroused him from his drunken stupor. He slid from his leather chair to the floor, and, tried to stand, but his legs were too numb from sitting. While he was on the floor, the room started spinning, he realized he was alone, and his family was not with him. No one was in the room with him. He must have been dreaming about them.

He could see from the floor his private line was blinking red, indicating that line had been called several times. The only ones to call his private line continuously would be Abigail or Sarah, his sweet little Sarah; she must be worried about her papa, and alarmed she couldn't reach him in the storm. Abigail's call would only be to inform him about where she had taken the children. This scenario of her leaving him and taking the children had played out several times over the course of their twenty-five years of marriage; with her threats of leaving and never coming back. She did leave once and took the children from their father for two whole years, and Addison knew she might do it again.

Abigail had watched her husband's excessive drinking increase over the years. His idle promises to stop drinking had gone nowhere. He told the children he could stop any time he wanted to, but he didn't want to. He would stop when he was ready. She had watched him losing his grip with reality since the storm in Australia. His quest was to figure out what happened to them on Kangaroo Island. Addison thought his wife and children weren't aware of his inquiries of the miraculous deliverance of his family on the island. She noticed his persistence and his pursuit of an explanation. Was it a miracle of God? She knew about the ongoing nightmares and about how he'd been crying out in his room, and screaming for his life.

As years passed, Abigail asked her husband if it was too hard to believe and conceive the truth about the God of the Bible. She could hardly get the question out of her mouth, before Addison filled the room with profanity. It was as though he was possessed. She had heard about demonic possession and Addison's reaction went far beyond an expected natural response. She wondered if she was actually looking at Satan himself?

Chapter Four: The Children

Abigail literally ran from her husband's presence. She had no idea about what might happen next. It took her husband months to recover from that episode, in fact he had to be hospitalized. It took him two years to regain Abigail's trust and her confidence to allow him to be alone with her and the children. In the meantime, while her husband was getting treatment for alcoholism and depression, Abigail took the children and moved to New York to be near her parents.

Sarah was the youngest of the three children. She had two older brothers, Joshua. and Michael. Abigail's parents were ecstatic to have their daughter and grandchildren relocated to New York City. The effects of aging was taking its toll on them both, and it was enjoyable having laughter in their home. Abigail's parents wanted Abigail to divorce Addison. He had fallen out of their favor long ago. Abigail refused, because of the children and their intertwined wealth. She felt relaxed being back in her parents' home, and thrilled to see the sheer joy on her children's faces. They were free for a time, not hearing or seeing the fighting between her and their father.

Addison remained in South Carolina undergoing treatment for depression, anxiety, and excessive drinking. He sent letters, cards, and presents and made telephones calls while they were in New York. His doctor's encouraged him not to visit his family or give false promises he was not ready to keep. The two year separation was healing for all, especially Abigail. Abigail's parents Jacob and Joanna Stein referred to Addison as functioning alcoholic with bipolar disorder. Abigail didn't want to hear her parents' diagnosis of her husband. She refused to accept her parent's theory. It was all Addison's fault. Abigail knew her parents were not telling the truth about his erratic behavior. Her parents had not faced up to the fact they all had a hand in destroying Addison Chandler. He was who he was partly, because of them. They wanted more than he could offer; they wanted him body and soul, and they all took it without worrying about the consequences.

Her parents said they were worried about Addison hurting her and the children emotionally or physically. They joked that they weren't concerned about raising a preoccupied, eccentric, egotistic daughter with no emotions. They were not in the dark that she was not capable of loving the suitors bidding for her heart. Her parents were convinced that James White was after their fortune. They realized Addison truly had fallen in love with their daughter. Abigail was emotionally crippled, because she wasn't able to trust. She was able to express emotions again after years of therapy from the kidnapping, and her parents stole that trust by separating her from James.

She felt Addison's love growing for her. The more he pursued her, the more she wanted to push the invisible dagger into his heart and destroy that love...and that she accomplished. She knew in the end he would hate her, because how could he love her when she couldn't even love herself? She remembered the night she ripped his heart out of his chest. She felt the sensation of ecstasy raging through her body, the euphoric feeling of destroying Addison was satisfying to her soul. She felt alive, because she felt his hurt and pain; she also felt his hatred when she walked out of the dining room. Her parents had spent thousands of dollars on psychiatrists, but no psychiatrist could ever help her, since she was separated from James. When her children were born, the ice started to melt from her cold heart.

Her parents weren't concerned about the excruciating pain Addison felt when he ran away for six months to get over her. Instead they bribed him by increasing her dowry after he did not attend the annual Black and White Ball. They were determined to reel him back in at any cost.

Her parents knew she was sick, and she knew it too. That was the difference between them. She knew the role she was playing in destroying Addison. It was for revenge because of her childhood being stolen from her and a love she would never have. Abigail knew from their first night as husband and wife she would suffer for destroying him.

Her parents were concerned, because their oldest grandson would be leaving home soon to study abroad, and his mother, younger brother and sister would be alone. Joshua and his brother Michael had often talked to their mother about her relationship with their father. Their concern was for her lack of safety if she went back to their father. In two years, Michael would be leaving home for school; their father could no longer intimidate them with his outrageous outbursts. They had become tall, strapping young men, and they no longer feared their father.

The tides had turned and Addison now feared his sons. He understood harm could come to him if they felt threatened by any of his actions toward their mother. His sons only tolerated him because of their mother; their love and respect had been destroyed years ago. Addison knew there was only one way he could ever restore his relationship with his sons and win back their affection, and that's only if God exists.

Joshua was ruthless like his father, but he protected his mother and siblings, regardless of how he treated others. Joshua didn't care if he lost his inheritance, because his father had taught him how to make money.

Michael was different, he wasn't as callous as his brother, and his hatred for his father was not as strong as Joshua. Michael had compassion. He understood that his father had a mental illness. His father was the Chief Financial Officer over a billion dollar enterprise, yet as Michael saw it, his father had no control over his personal life due to his alcohol consumption? Addison and Abigail's children weren't aware of the demons their parents were dealing with. The demons that were eating them alive and destroying them both was anger and the spirit of unforgiveness. Addison did not mask his hatred for Abigail. She had practiced being plastic her entire life. She got under her husband's skin by acting as though he didn't exist. Her father called her china doll for a reason. Her parents knew she was ice cold. They tried to help her with psychiatrists, jewelry, and extravagant vacations, but nothing worked. Her parents knew deep down inside that they were both miserable, and they were determined to inflict suffering on each other.

Jacob and Joann Stein knew their grandchildren were heaven sent, but they always wondered how they were conceived. How could this happen, since neither Addison nor Abigail ever showed any love or affection towards one another? They had not been known to share a bedroom in the twenty five years of their marriage.

The Stein's wanted to ask their daughter if the children were conceived by artificial insemination. They didn't put it past their daughter; they knew their daughter was eccentric, since the kidnapping and loss of her only love, but she was their only child and one day she and her children would inherit all they owned. They were thrilled to observe that the children were normal, intelligent and well behaved. They knew Joshua would manage the bulk of their fortune, because, like his father he was a shrewd businessman.

Sarah had a peculiar way of thinking she could read people's minds, but that was nothing for them to be concerned about. She was a lovely child, always concerned for the welfare of others. Sarah was very mature for her age, and had inherited her mother's beauty. With all the drama surrounding their parents they were happy that, the grandchildren had turned out quite well. Although Addison Chandler had lost favor in their eyes, they still felt he was a good fit for Abigail.

Thirteen year old Sarah loved and respected her father. She had always been able to see beyond the hurt and pain.

Nancy was Sarah's nurse from birth, due to her mother's postpartum depression, and she stayed on as her nanny till Sarah was ten. Nancy explained to Sarah what her name meant in the Bible, and she often quoted scripture to her. She usually did this when she knew no one was at home, or when she took Sarah to the park or on an outing. Her father made each of her nannies sign a contract that they would not teach his children any of their religious beliefs. He did not want his children's heads filled with foolishness.

Addison was convinced he was an atheist; because of the pain he endured at the hands of a deranged mother, who claimed to know God. In order to protect himself, he had to stop believing what he had been taught about God.

Addison foolishly pursued worldly success, because he couldn't believe God could put an end to his suffering. When he grew into a young man, he took control of his own destiny.

Addison acknowledged Abigail had given him three healthy beautiful children. His attitude was "Call me when it's all over, and she's back in her room with the baby." He had no desire to see his wife in pain. In fact, he tried to convince her to have their children by cesarean section; that way he could select the date each child would be born and wouldn't have to wait for hours for the baby to come. Usually he didn't get to the hospital till after she delivered. He didn't care about the risks for Abigail to have their children by cesarean section. Addison was trying to have control over nature, but Abigail put her foot down and was adamant that she was not having an unnecessary cesarean.

Chapter Five: The Employees

The sirens were blaring. The storm must be getting worse, Addison thought as the sirens increased in intensity. It didn't matter to Addison, because he was safe in his Ivory tower. He had everything he needed in his office, food, water and cognac. What more did a man need? He was too drunk to want the company of a woman. He knew if he picked up the telephone and called one of his escort services, they would go through hell even in this storm to get someone to his office. Addison laughed to himself at the thought of fools who would die to make a dollar.

Addison took a long swig of the Cognac as his mind drifted off to the day that Ann Northup was ushered into his office. He was immediately impressed; he never could conceal his admiration for a beautiful woman. Ann was wearing a Coco Chanel tailored suit in purity white, and she knew she looked stunning. Her appearance was pristine and professional. The money she spent on finishing school and executive classes was a worthwhile investment, and she received her return tenfold.

Addison Chandler was so awestruck; he could barely speak. He struggled to find the right words, "Mrs. Northup, what a pleasure to meet you in person. "I've read your professional resumes and your accomplishments are outstanding for someone so young."

"I must make one correction," she said. "You called me Mrs. Northup, its Ms. Northup."

Addison apologized.

He hesitated, but decided to ask the question. "Would you call yourself a team player Ms. Northup?"

"No I'm not Mr. Chandler. I was raised an only child and I did not have to compete with siblings; therefore, I was born to lead, and my father raised me that way."

Mr. Chandler, if you're looking for a team player I'm not the executive for this position. "However, if you want an independent, well-organized, analytical person to get the job done, I'm your new Vice President."

"Ms. Northup, welcome to Chandler Brokerage Firm."

It had been twenty five years since he'd met another china doll. Ann walked out of his office the same way his wife had walked out of the dining room so many years ago. What misery would this china doll bring him? Would he wind up hating Ann as much as he despised his wife?

Addison was reliving the last twenty five years of his marriage? Is it possible this might be his last night on earth? He had often heard people say your life flashes before your eyes before you die. He knew he was drunk enough to die tonight, if the hurricane didn't take him first.

Addison was trying to see the time on his watch, but his eyes were unable to focus. To him it seemed like he had been in his offices for days. He began to slip back down memory lane, and laughed out loud as he thought about his wife's threats to have the liquor cabinet and the wine cellar permanently sealed off in his office and their home. When they discussed building a new home, Abigail insisted there would be no plans for a liquor cabinet or wine cellar in the architectural plans. She had enough of Addison's drinking. He couldn't find happiness. He had worldly possessions, but he was empty and lost, He was a drunk in a hurricane, in an office building alone. He had not found satisfaction in life, not even with his family, except for Sarah.

Sarah was different. Nancy, Sarah's nanny had a significant influence on Sarah. Sarah had fallen in love with Jesus, the Son of God. She found God to be loving and compassionate. Who else would sacrifice His only Son for her family and others families to have eternal life?

Sarah found comfort in prayer, when she would hear her mother and father arguing over him coming home drunk. Nancy assured her that God was in control, no matter what she thought or how she felt.

Addison and Abigail felt at home in South Carolina, but Abigail knew that if the marriage was to last, they needed a change of scenery and a brand new start. Addison owned the largest and most successful brokerage firm in the Carolinas; there were no limits to his purchasing power. The alcohol had consumed the relationships with his wife, children and friends; but his business had continued to thrive thanks to his ability to hire the best and brightest.

Addison was speaking gibberish, "Let me die; let it all be over with; I don't want to go on," he moaned as he remembered all of the lives he had destroyed. He was obsessed and fixated on knowing everything about everyone and about everything in their personal lives. Addison wanted to know if they too were hiding the pain of their childhood, and if their past had been dark and as painful as his own. His thoughts were consumed with who they were, and what had happened in their childhood. Addison wanted intimate details on his employees. Tonight, it felt like his employee's were haunting him and his memories. The employees were not willing to let him be free. He felt like Ebenezer Scrooge, with his cold-heart, a man who despised seeing people happy. The details he wanted, he had no business knowing, and these ghosts were coming to get their pound of flesh. The details of his employee's personal lives were crying out to him. Usually the alcohol would deaden the signals to his brain, but not tonight. Addison visualized himself being dragged down a tunnel to the board room to be confronted by his demons.

Ann Northup was guaranteed a position at Chandler Brokerages Firm. Addison was proud of his record of hiring the best and brightest from top Ivy League Schools. Ann had done her undergraduate degree at Brown and her Master's and Doctorate at Harvard, and had graduated Magna Cum Laude. Addison knew her dress size, shoes size and credit score before she ever stepped foot in his firm. He knew she had been orphaned at an early age. He was intrigued by the fact that she had never had a boyfriend or dated and that she was a twenty-three year old virgin. Addison's corporate offices had the best private detectives and the best personality tests money could buy. He made sure his employees took these test so that he would know their personality types. Addison told himself he needed these details up front, in order to know what he was dealing with, and to determine if they were a fit for his firm. The reality was that the tests were given to his employees to see who would be his next victim, since he saw his employees as his personal property.

The private detective had overlooked one important piece of information; he had not established Ann's doctoral connection to the Harvard personality tests Addison's firm had purchased. Her background check indicated, she had worked with a group of doctoral students experimenting with personality profiles, but he didn't know she was the one responsible for these tests for Fortune 500 companies. Ann had noticed the trend where companies tried to figure out employee's personality. Fortune 500 companies were interested in how to retain their executives. It was huge expense for companies to negotiate for an executive only to find out six months later, they were not a good fit.

The Harvard Personality Test was an independent project Ann took on with some of her doctoral colleagues on their own time. She and a few grad students compiled data and sold it to the Fortune 500 companies. The corporations accepted these tests as evidence that the employees they would be hiring would be a good fit for their company. Ann and the other women in the group used the test to see if women could command a higher compensation package, and it worked. The corporate world was cut-throat, and the women crafters of the test were aware that they were generally offered less valuable compensation packages in comparison to their less qualified and less educated male counterparts. Ann had been taught her value by her father while growing up. Her father would tell her,

"One day you will be worth millions to your husband, if you stay pure." She knew her father had it wrong. Ann understood that she was beautiful and intelligent, and she knew how to negotiate her own salary, stock options, bonuses and salary increases based on her performance. She didn't need a man to dictate that to her. She would find a man to marry who would be the father to her children. Her qualifications for her suitor were that he had to be intelligent, handsome and love children. She would choose him, and not the other way around. Ann was in no rush; she had time and youth on her side. She was twenty-three years old and had given herself five years; before she would be ready to start a family. She knew that once she had children, they would be her career. As a wealthy woman with options, she would occupy herself with charitable endeavors that would make her look good and keep her busy once the children were in school.

Ann had planned her life around having children and already had their schedules in place. They would be involved in hiking, swimming, skiing, soccer, gymnastics, tennis and horseback riding. Her parents could not do these activities with her as a child; they could only watch because they were too old to participate. All of this was so far in the past. Why did she still get upset at her parents lack of participation?

Chapter Six: Commanding the Room

Addison opened his top draw and took out another bottle of Remy Martin. Remy, a spirit that always made him feel better about life. At that moment, twenty-five year old Neal Newman entered his office.

Addison asked Neal, "Have you seen the new employee, she started this morning. Her name is Ann Northup and she's beautiful and smart. She's not married, and according to our background check, she's never dated. She has brains and beauty, and that's a great combination to have. I may have just hired your wife, Neal."

"Not me boss, I'm not the marrying type." Neal responded. "I haven't sowed my wild oats yet; and any way who wants one woman, when I can have as many as I want, maybe even a hundred."

Addison looked at him with saddened eyes, as he took another sip of his drink. "It may be fun when it starts out, but after a while even the most beautiful woman loses her luster. If you don't have the woman with that special connection who makes you feels you're the only man in the world. The one who's gray hair and the wrinkles only make her more beautiful in your sight, because you loved her for years and never noticed her aging. You don't want to think about whose arms she's been in, or the smell of another man's scent on her body." Addison digressed.

He continued, "People are fooled into thinking soap and water will wash the scent of sin off the body; it doesn't."

Neal looked at Addison, and for a moment he felt pity for him. He was one of the wealthiest men he knew, yet it was obvious he wasn't happy. He had a beautiful wife, three intelligent children and a successful business, yet here he is sitting drinking himself into a stupor before lunch time.

Addison announced, "We're having a board meeting this morning to introduce our new Global Vice President of Finance."

"Is it Ms. Ann Northup?" Neal responded.

"I'm impressed, you remember her name." Addison quipped.

"Yes, I'm impressed myself; let's get to the board room."

As they walked down the hall, Neal noticed the extravagance of the office furnishing. The Paintings alone must have cost Addison a fortune. The marble and mahogany tables were exquisite and the leather chairs in the boardroom felt as though you were sinking into a cloud.

The company's vice presidents and department heads were already seated, as Addison and Neal entered the room. Neal was envied by every male in the boardroom, because he seemed to be in Addison's good graces, and to have his undivided attention. Neal was the up and coming star at Chandler's Brokerage Firm, handpicked by Addison himself. In the end what price would Neal have to pay to be the golden child? It had been rumored Addison's last protégé committed suicide;

he couldn't live with the intrusiveness of constantly being spied on in his personal life.

Ann Northup was as much intimidating as she was breathtaking. Her mere presence commanded the atmosphere as though she already owned the company when she walked into the boardroom. The men in the room took a deep breath; the women began adjusting their clothing.

The women in the room admired her confidence, as she was introduced to the board members and department heads. Ann made mental a note of the reactions to the announcement of her being named Global Vice President of Finance.

Her classes in psychology had taught her to pay attention to people's behavior and body language, which had given her an advantage over her colleagues. Neal bit his lip, as he was being introduced, "She's more than beautiful, she's drop dead gorgeous. No wonder Addison needed a drink after she left his office."

The men in the boardroom were trying to hold it together as best they could; they had turned into fifteen year old boys, seeing a beautiful girl for the first time. The grins on their faces were embarrassing, including Neal's.

Ann was accustomed to this type of greeting. She was polite and cordial as everyone introduced themselves and gave their names, departments, and titles. She could not help but notice Neal Newman, especially since Neal did not give his name or title. In her endearing voice she asked, "And your name?"

He smiled, "Neal Newman, I'm Mr. Chandler's apprentice in training for partnership." She smiled, making a mental note and thinking, "Husband material." Ann was looking at her future husband, and Neal would be filed under "future plans," since she had five years to accomplish her goals. She had plenty of time to stake her claim on Mr. Neal Newman.

Ann imagined that Neal couldn't be more than twenty-five. In five years, he would be still young enough to start a family and participate in parenting their children. Standing in front of her was the whole package. She could perceive from his annunciation that he was well-educated.

Ann was from a middle class family; her mother was a teacher, and her father an accountant, which gave them a comfortable lifestyle, plus Ann's grandmother had left her mother a decent inheritance. Her parents invested in a private school education for her. They wanted her to have the best education money could buy. They were not religious people, but they did believe in being good people. They did not lie, steal or cheat to get ahead in life. To them good morals and hard work was important. They wanted Ann to remain a virgin. Her father felt this would be a valuable virtue and guarantee her a husband from any Ivy League school. He would say men didn't want used goods, especially in a wife. He'd share stories about how his colleagues loved bragging about how their wife was a virgin on their wedding night. Her father highly prized her virginity, and would tell her that her value was better than rubies.

Ann's father did not understand that she would not keep her virginity because of him or any other man. She would keep possession of her virginity; because she valued herself. She understood the psychology her father was trying to use with these stories. Ann would be worth millions regardless. The Ivy League Schools she attended used the same propaganda her father used, in trying to encourage the female students to keep the code of honor, so that they'd be chosen when men were looking for a wife. They told them stories of how men's parents would hire private investigators to do background checks into young ladies personal lives', before they would allow their sons to be engaged. It didn't matter how beautiful or how educated a girl was, and it didn't even matter if the family was wealthy; they still wanted to know that their sons were getting a virgin. Ivy League women were taught that their virginity brought financial wealth to the husband, and could even securing a position for him in any Fortune 500 company. People were unaware of the young women that had gone through Ivy League schools who had paid their way as high class escorts. Ann's father always reminded her to never forget what he was telling her. "Once you give it away, you can never get it back," he'd explain. Ann promised herself, she would keep her virginity for herself, not for her husband.

The school and her father were both hypocritical and only preaching to one side of the choir. These kinds of things were never said to Ivy League men. "Did they think we never discussed celibacy with our male classmates?," Ann thought.

When she brought up the issue of purity with her father, he explained that men didn't have to wait, simply because they were men. He capped off his explanation by saying telling Ann that smart men waited though. From a young age, Ann came to an understanding of the double standard for men and women.

Chapter Seven: Focused & Driven

Addison's daughter, Sarah, wondered why her father had not tried to call to let his family know he was safe. He lacked good sense at times and especially if he was drinking. There was an elite group of businessmen in his company, who felt they were superior to the rest of the partners. Those who felt they were superior, would dismiss the other six partners who had affiliations with organized religion. It didn't matter what their belief system or rituals were, they were all lumped into one category. The elites would consume Addison's favorite drinks, Cognac or Scotch. Even those who didn't normally drink, still indulged in order to be a part of her father's inner circle.

Sarah had witnessed her father hysterically laughing, and calling the rejected partners names, as he imagined them on their knees, praying to their gods. Addison would tell the group that they were praying to themselves instead of to an unseen deity.

Once Addison announced to everyone in the boardroom, that he attributed his success and the success of the firm to their effort and loyalty to him. He laughed, and said they should all be bowing down to me. I am the one who made them all filthy rich; not their invisible god's.

"What had their god's given any of them?"

"I'm their god; they're all crazy," he cackled.

Addison allowed them to have their god's, because he understood that they needed something other than themselves to believe in. He could not argue with the fact that they had made the firm money and had built great relationships worldwide.

Addison had his Cognac, and they had their gods. His companies and properties grew and expanded because of them; the revenue and profits were proof of that.

The company's success had caused much scrutiny and financial audits by the Internal Revenue Service (IRS) over the last five years, but the IRS never prevailed, because Addison hired the top accounting firms in the state of South Carolina. Addison threatened to call the Government Accounting Office to have a forensic audit on the IRS for the misappropriation of taxpayers' dollars on these ridiculous audits. He felt his company was being unduly targeted, and he was sure his competitors were using the IRS against him as a business tactic to bring down his firm.

Five years quickly passed in what seemed liked months. Ann was focused on her career and earning a million dollars before age 30. Her goal was not solely to be wealthy on paper; she wanted money in the bank. She enjoyed watching her 401k and her stock options grow, and there was nothing like feeling cash in her hand. Many of Ann's colleagues relied on their 401k and company stock, but she knew that could be risky. The stock market had collapsed before, and it could happen again. There was nothing to guarantee another crash wouldn't happen. Ann had the intelligence to know how to manage money, invest it, and make it grow. She lived up to her title as head of finance. It was her responsibility to inform her colleagues' of standard bank practices on deposits and the insurance coverage limit. She knew that putting their money in one bank was not smart, since they are only insured for $250,000 per depositor. Ann was astonished when checking company investment portfolio's at how many millionaires didn't know this information. She thought, "Banks are not going to provide this kind of unsolicited information to investors. They're in the business of making money through lending from the bank accounts of others. Wealthy people can't expect them to cut into their own profits that way."

Neal was now Senior Vice Presidents of Chandler's brokerage firm in the marketing division. Addison reserved the title of President only for himself, so no division heads got the title of president. He said there was one President of Chandler Brokerage Firm, and it was him.

Neal and Ann's wedding date was set for

July 4, 1997. It had been five years since Ann walked into Addison Chandler's office, on July 7, 1992. In the five years at Chandler, their lives were entangled with lies and deceit. Ann was a master money manager, she was skilled at investing, borrowing, lending, budgeting, saving and forecasting. Her knowledge of International banking made her highly sought-after, globally. She was not one to be dismissed on any level. Ann was Neal's equal, if not his superior. She was driven for success and Neal would be an asset to her future plans. That's why she had chosen him from the first day she saw him in the boardroom. Neal also sensed from their first encounter that she would change his life for the better. He didn't know how or when, but he knew from the first day in the boardroom, from the determined look on her face, Ann Northup had chosen him, and he knew it would be on her terms and not his.

Ann had a sixth sense for merging companies and knowing which companies to bring into Chandler's portfolio. Her mergers would go through without a hitch. It was becoming increasing uncomfortable for Neal to be in the board meeting. She was the superstar of the company and soon to be his wife. He was privy to information he hadn't shared with her concerning the six partners, which met privately. She didn't know that Neal was being groomed and polished as Addison's replacement as President of Chandler Brokerage Firm. Had she known, maybe she would have cared about the good old boys, and what they did in their meetings. The men were playing childish games, while drinking and thinking of ways to keep her and the other female executives from becoming CEO. Chandler definitely had their glass ceiling, males only attitude.

Ann used her time wisely, studying and learning international trade. She had taken The Chandler Corporation global, and the company now had international recognition. The good old boys club reveled in the idea that the world had to come to them.

Ann purposely refused to date Neal for the first four years of her employment at Chandler. She didn't want love to interfere with her goals and she was determined to stay focused and keep her promise to herself concerning her virginity. There was no disputing the fact that Neal was handsome and had the body of a Greek God. She was taking no chances at having a weak moment of temptation and pleasure. She knew she was the topic of the company's water cooler talk; because of her refusing to date and her decision to abstain from sex until marriage. Addison made sure this information circulated around the office. This demonstrated his immaturity and childish ways. When he was drunk he often obsessed over how he had been unable to break her spirit and make her resign. The reason he tried to force her to resign was because his business acquaintances would ask for Ann before asking for him. It was as though he worked for her, and not the other way around.

Her female colleagues found it puzzling that a woman in modern society would want to keep her virginity. They couldn't help but notice her beauty and marveled at the thought that she would not want to give herself to a man, especially a fine specimen like Neal. They couldn't believe a woman as beautiful as Ann could be as dedicated to her career as she was.

While the office ladies were gossiping at the water-cooler, Ann was stock piling money for her future and the future of her children. She knew Neal could comfortably provide for her and the family they would have together, but Ann was not satisfied with that. She wanted to establish generational wealth. Addison hated that about Ann. He resented the fact that he couldn't bring her off her high horse no matter how hard he tried. She was always one step ahead of him, and her work ethic was impeccable. He could find nothing to challenge her on. He found no fault with her work. Addison had been down this rabbit hole before, as he tried to find fault with his wife, Abigail. He had stooped so low as to have Ann's telephone bugged at her condo. He wanted to know if there was a world of Ann Northup outside the office. Unable to dig up any dirt after three years, he ceased the surveillance on her and turned his attention to harassing Neal, and pushing to know when his marriage to Ann would take place, and why he hadn't gotten her into bed. Addison yelled at Neal, "She's only a woman; drug her, do whatever you have to!" Neal finally found the courage to tell him, "You've crossed the line; she's going to be my wife in a few days, and this obsession you have with her has to stop. Addison, what is It?" At that moment in the sickness and darkness of his mind, he realized that he wanted Ann.

Neal went on to ask, "Why are you trying to destroy her and her reputation?" Addison was insanely jealous of Ann's success in his company. He wanted her dethroned and brought down to his level, having no morals and no superiority over him or his company. He wanted her to drown in his cesspool, with the rest of his employees who blindly followed his orders. He had no control over Ann. He had never been able to intimidate her, and this infuriated him. He knew she was not religious, therefore he knew her morals had nothing to do with her belief in God. He had men following her for years, since he was determined to know his employee's weaknesses. His obsession with Ann didn't stop there; he knew when she had her monthly menstrual cycle. Even with all his private detectives Addison would never know about her promise to herself and her father. She never shared this information with anyone. It wasn't difficult keeping the details of her life concealed, since she didn't have time for friends. They were only a distraction. In the past year she had finally allowed Neal to take her on a couple of dates, since she knew it was time to get to know the man she was planning to marry. She knew Neal was seeing other women, but it was okay with her, since they were not in an exclusive relationship. She would save that for six months before the wedding. At that point he would be exclusively dating her.

It amused Ann that men felt they needed sexual gratification. It would be so much safer to get that release from masturbating. That way they could alleviate the possibility of getting sexually transmitted diseases. She was not worried about Neal contracting any sexual transmitted diseases since Addison's company policy was that all single people in the company had to be tested monthly for infections and sexual transmitted diseases. This was another reason Addison was outraged with Ann. She did not have to be tested, because she wasn't dating. He tried to get company policy changed to include non-dating employees, but his attorneys convinced him to abandon this idea. They knew that if they attempted this Ann would file a major lawsuit against the company and would win.

Ann didn't like distractions, or people wasting her time, and dating was a waste of time, to her. To Ann, a relaxing evening wasn't sitting around listening to idle chatter with a wine glass in one hand. Gossiping was a waste of her time. If she couldn't make money with the information, it was of no value to her. A relaxing evening to Ann, was to sitting in her comfortable ocean view condo reading and learning new strategies for making money.

Chapter Eight: The Wedding

Ann had acquired two environmental companies for Chandler. These companies were making millions of dollars from energy upgrades for new home buyers and builders, which they really didn't need. Ann, with her psychology background, knew that the majority of people would believe whatever you wanted them to believe, as long as you used repetition on them. This was why Neal's marketing department was successful. He was able to convince the ad agency to accept his ideas, and give them to the public. Investors, homeowners and state officials were quick to believe they had to be in on the upcoming development in residential and commercial properties.

The average person is content to be told how to think rather than reading a book and educating themselves. Ann knew the average citizen did not realize they could request the minutes from their local, state and national governments to see how their tax dollars were being spent. Most people did not bother to request the budgets and salaries of their elected officials. In her opinion, they needed to educate themselves and be responsible for learning which bills were being passed and written in their cities and states, as well as at the Federal level. She was surprised when she was in public and would hear people complaining about tax bills that were being passed. All of this was public knowledge, but the public officials knew the average citizen was not going to make the effort to be informed. This was one way Addison and his corporations made money off the backs of hard working people. People were too tired to read after a long day's work. All they wanted was a hot meal and the comfort of relaxing in their favor chair. One reason corporations felt they were superior to the masses was because people are ill informed. Therefore, through ads they would tell the masses what they needed, and information on an as needed basis.

Ann knew that knowledge was power, and the more knowledge she had the more powerful she was. She was a force to be reckoned with, especially at the Chandler company. She loved the taste of power, and she had given herself five years to drink of this cup, and the taste was addicting.

Ann was on a countdown to her wedding day, and she had allowed her imagination the opportunity to day dream about becoming Mrs. Neal Newman. At night she would lie awake wondering if he was thinking of her. She had been hard on Neal over the years, but she felt it was necessary. Soon Neal would have her all to himself, and she would no longer have to be at war with Addison Chandler. She would leave Addison and his company, to become the wife of Neal Newman. Ann was thrilled at the idea of marrying the man she loved. She was ready to start her family, and hoped to get pregnant on her wedding night.

One night, Ann dreamed about an angel her mother had told her about before she was born. The angel stood behind her father in her mother's hospital room, after her mother was rushed to the hospital when she became violently ill. That's when her mother found out she was five months pregnant. In her dream, the angel was trying to talk to her, but she couldn't understand the language he was speaking. The harder she tried to understand what he was saying, the larger the angel grew. In the background, she could hear her mother saying, "Ann, the angel's language is not for you to understand." When she awoke she was perplexed and wondering what the dream meant. She had never had this dream before, and it seemed to make no sense.

Ann's mother told her the stories when she was a child, but she had never asked her mother what the angel represented. Ann had written the date of the dream in her journal.

As her wedding date approached, Addison used every weapon in his arsenal to try and control Ann and Neal's wedding, but she was not going to tolerate any of his foolishness, or even permit him to see the wedding announcements until he received one in the mail.

Addison was furious. Ann did not allow Addison to give Neal a bachelor party, because she felt they were childish and disrespectful to the bride. Addison wanted to walk Ann down the aisle, since her father was deceased, but she decided to walk down the aisle alone. After her parent's death, Ann decided she would not have a traditional wedding. The only one she wanted to see at the altar was Neal.

Everyone in Neal's family was not happy to see her marry him, especially his older brother, John, who felt Ann was too controlling. John told Neal he was marrying a female version of Addison Chandler. He tried to convince Neal that a woman, who would not allow her fiancé to sleep with her before the wedding was not normal. He asked Neal, "If you don't try the goods out first, how do you know if you'll like them?" Neal felt John was being ridiculous. He knew his brother was jealous of Ann, because she had her own money. John was also jealous of Neal's success as Senior Vice President, but didn't have the courage to tell his brother the truth, so he went behind Neal's back and asked Ann to do a merger for his company with one of Chandler's companies. Ann refused to do the merger, because John's company was not financially solid. Since then, John resented Ann. She never told Neal, about his request because it was a business deal and it had nothing to do with Neal or his marketing department.

Ann was happy to know that Neal's parents were in agreement with the wedding, even if John wasn't. Neal's parents wanted him to be happy, and even the expense of the wedding didn't matter to Robert and Gale Newman. Although, they chided with him that he should have gone to City Hall to get married for twenty-five dollars; that would have saved them the expense of a big elaborate wedding.

Ann explained to his parents that she ruled out the traditional wedding, because she didn't want anyone to feel as if they were an unwanted guest. It was open seating. No tables were reserved, and the guests who arrived early would get the best seats. She planned to make sure there was seating for Neal's parents.

She got the idea for a non-traditional wedding on her first cruise, while on deck all guests are equal. The only tipping for the waiters had to be done on the passenger's credit cards issued by the cruise ship. This ensured that the person tipping a hundred dollars received the same service as the person tipping ten dollars.

There was no formal dress code for the wedding; her guest could dress as they saw fit. Her colleagues were well aware of her high standards, and they would never embarrass themselves by attending a formal function without being properly dressed. She overheard the women in the VIP lounge talking about their designer dresses, and she smiled at their desire to impress her.

There was a rumor that a former employee once showed up at a co-workers wedding in designer blue jeans. He was a young preppy type, and was escorted out of the gala by Addison Chandler himself. To make his point about the importance of formality, Addison sent his termination notice by text.

Ann really didn't care what anyone wore to her wedding. She just wanted the day to be fun, relaxing and full of laughter. She didn't even care if Neal showed up in a pair of Versace shorts and stood at her side as she showed off her Vera Wang wedding gown.

Ann believed it was ineffective to tell people what to do; the wiser strategy was to encourage people to expect more of themselves. The wedding was on July 4th, and since the guests were all staying at the hotel they could easily return to their rooms to change clothes.

When some of the women at the office received their invitations, they wanted to know what they should wear. Ann suspected that based on their history of never attending any of the company's formal events, none of the women would attend. They were invited, but she guessed they stayed away because they felt they didn't fit in. They were asking either to be nosey and to have something to talk about around the water cooler, or simply to find a reason to count themselves out.

Ann was directly responsible for hiring at least 300 employees; not counting the staff in the satellite offices. She could not have grown the global finance operation without great employees. She wanted them to feel like family at her wedding, and she hoped to show them she wasn't an ice fairy that lived in a castle with a heart of stone.

On July 4th at 4:00 PM, she would become Mrs. Ann Northup Newman. Ann didn't tell Neal, she planned to leave her position at Chandler's once they married, but she looked forward to telling Addison Chandler where to go. He had done everything in his power to make her life a living hell for the last five years, and she was determined he would never win. He could never defeat her with his narcissistic head games. It didn't matter the cost, he just wanted to win. Addison's wires became crossed, to the extent that he treated her like she was his. When he argued with her, it was as if he was fighting Abigail through Ann. It wasn't about love, intimacy or a sense of deep connection to his wife or Ann. He was trying to exchange Abigail for Ann. He refused to meet Abigail's needs; therefore he could not meet Ann's need for respect either. Addison was sick, and everyone around him knew it, except him. His psychiatrist had talked to both Abigail and Ann to try and explain the confused state of Addison's mind. Abigail was curious about why Ann stayed with Addison's Firm. Ann's credentials and achievement were so obvious that the corporate hounds were aggressively pursuing her. Why had she endured Addison's narcissistic ways all these years?

Ann had her own personal reasons why she had not left the firm. Chandler had gone global and she wanted the recognition that she deserved as a female with the firm. She was a global player in the world of global finance. She survived five years as a Senior Vice President in a male-dominated field.

Addison could turn on the charm when needed, and over the years Ann came to understand that he was a narcissist. Most of Addison's condition was due to his environment, his drinking, and his genetic disposition. Ann was unaffected by his cruelty, since she knew he could not find fault with her work. She was one step ahead of every trap he set for her. She learned his habits and how he acted after he'd been drinking. Ann knew a narcissist would never harm themselves. When Addison had his narcissistic outbursts, whoever was nearby would receive his wrath. Attacking others was his way of hiding his own inadequacies and the inability to be critical of himself. Today, all of Addison's sick narcissistic games will be dumped back in his own lap, and he will get to choke on his own words, Ann thought.

Ann and Neal requested no wedding gifts; they wanted all monetary gifts to go to charity. All they needed was each other. All of the arrangements for the wedding were taken care of by Julia, the wedding planner. Ann told her what she wanted, and Julia made sure everything was perfect. No matter how much Addison Chandler tried to bribe or threaten her, she stood firm.

Ann and Neal decided they didn't need a prenuptial agreement. Their children would be well provided for, no matter what unforeseen circumstances might take place in the future. They had also taken precautions to protect their assets from the whims and insanity of Addison Chandler.

Neal had not been totally honest with Ann regarding his relationships with other women, which is why he never pressured her into having sex. However, he did show her that he could be romantic by showering her with cards, flowers, candy and his original poetry.

Neal had only one request for their wedding; he wanted them to say their own vows to each other before being pronounced man and wife. Ann agreed to his request, "Well of course we can say our vows to each other, but only if you write a book of poetry." She loved

Neal's poetry, and this was her way of squeezing more sweet words out of him.

He laughed at the suggestion, "Are you kidding me? We get married in two days. I only have one day to get this done, my future wife." Ann wanted to have the poems published and bound in a leather book, and presented to him as a surprise wedding gift on their honeymoon.

Chapter Nine: The Biggest Merger

Their honeymoon destination was top secret. Neither of them wanted unwelcomed guests. Addison, and Neal's brother John, could find anybody, no matter how remote the island, but she did not plan to make it easy for them. They would have to use man hours, planes, boats and satellites to track them down.

They wanted to be alone after five long years of waiting. Their marriage would be Ann's biggest merger, and this one was for the rest of their lives. After all, she would be giving someone her body and her soul for the first time.

Addison and John were irate that there was not going to be a wedding party. "Who's heard of such a thing, no flower girls, no maid of honor and most of all no best man?" John told Addison.

Addison responded, "She's not even allowing anyone to give a toast to the bride and groom!"

Addison and John were scheming about how they could commandeer the stage after the ceremony. They were so undone, they even hinted at having the Ritz-Carlton burned to the ground. Neither of them were thinking rationally, because they had not been included.

Ann knew the lengths to which these two would go, so she was taking no chances and decided to hire security for the wedding. The security team was instructed that once the ceremony was over, all audio equipment was to be removed from the ballroom and patio, giving no one a chance to make a public announcement for the bride and groom. The music was pre-recorded and closely guarded. Ann had to stay two steps ahead of John and Addison; they were perplexed and she imagined that they could be extremely sinister, and she would do damage control, to guard against any potential plot they might dream up. They would stop at nothing to bring Ms. Ann Northup down off of her high horse. She was winning, and they didn't like it.

July 4th was a perfect day for a wedding in Columbia, South Carolina. Severe thunderstorms were predicted. Thunderstorms were always possible this time of year in Columbia, so she had a backup plan in the event of inclement weather. If a thunderstorm occurred, the wedding would be in the ballroom. If the weather was pleasant, it would take place in the garden. They were expecting 500 guests, most of them had arrived the night before the wedding.

Neal and Ann had been communicating by telephone. They had decided not to see each other until the wedding day. Neal teased Ann, saying "You made me wait five years, three more days means nothing." She didn't know where Neal was staying. She was at the Ritz-Carlton in the bridal suite. The luxurious suite included his and her bath and bedrooms, and the honeymoon suite was on the top floor, overlooking the whole city. The view was breathtaking.

The Honeymoon suite looked as though they had stepped back into the Victorian era, with Queen Victoria and her Prince Consort. The décor did not suit either Ann or Neal's preferences, but The Ritz was very accommodating and in three days the honeymoon suite was transformed into a dreamland of roses. The room was to be dismantled and returned to its original state as soon as they left; if any pictures of the room were leaked to the press by the Ritz-Carlton, their contract insured that they would be handsomely compensated and the hotel risked an enormous lawsuit. The room was swept clean of video and recording devices, and the location of some of their guests were closely guarded. They wanted to prevent Addison's global competitors from infiltrating as caterers, housecleaning staff and delivery drivers. They would exploit whatever opportunities they could to find careless employees.

The past six months had been intriguing and exciting. She appreciated the opportunity to get acquainted with Neal on a more intimate level, not as his colleague or competitor, but as his wife. There were those who viewed Ann as heartless for keeping Neal on ice for 4½ years. For the most part, they kept their distance from one another, aside from business trips and things like that. Ann made it a point to never put herself in a compromising position, or to even have physical contact; even holding hands and kissing was out of the question. From the moment they met, Neal and Ann knew they were meant for each other.

A month after they met, they ended up in Hong Kong on a business trip together. Addison had not informed either of them that they would both be on the trip. Addison and Neal made the trip in Addison's private jet; Addison said it was training for Neal. Addison's secretary had booked Ann on a commercial fight. She was there for a merger. They were all staying at the Four Season's Hotel in Hong Kong. Addison thought he could get under Ann's skin; by booking her reservations in business class, but his plan failed, because she always upgraded herself to first class. Amanda, Ann's secretary, knew to change her accommodations. Once Amanda saw that Ann was booked at the Four Season's in Hong Kong, she knew the reservation were fine because Ann had stayed there before, and she knew which room to reserve for her.

Neal's room was on the same floor; and after they bumped into one another in the hallway, they decided to have dinner together, without Addison. Addison was furious with Neal, and on the second day of the trip, Neal accidently left his cell phone in the hotel, and this infuriated Addison even more. Addison had security go into Neal's room when he could not get in touch with him, and that's how he knew Neal had left his phone and wasn't lying to him.

Addison had planned an evening for them with geisha girls, and despite being upset, it didn't stop his wild night of partying and drinking. Neal knew he would pay for leaving his phone, but he didn't care. He was in the moment, and at that moment, all he could think about was Ann. He was intoxicated with her; and the soft lighting in the lounge made her look like a Greek goddess. Her beauty and charm aroused him in a way he had never felt before; it was as if she wasn't real. Neal wished he could capture that moment in time. He wished time could stand still, so that the beauty of the moment could last a life time. They ate their dinner in complete silence. The did not want to rush the evening. A sense of camaraderie flowed between them and they felt they could read each other's mind.

Neal and Ann were enjoying each other company so much that neither one realized they had stayed up all night talking and laughing. When Neal noticed the time on his watch he said, "Wow, 6:06 a.m. Addison's jet would be leaving at 7:30 a.m." He had to get back to his hotel and pack. "Relax Neal", Ann whispered, "I can take care of it; I'll call Armada. She'll make sure your luggage is at Hong Kong International straight to the private hanger, and you can meet Addison when he arrives." Neal was impressed Ann was beautiful, smart, and in less than twenty four hours they had they both explained what they wanted to accomplish in the next five years.

Neal was quick to tell Ann that marriage was not in his five year plan, but if he had a change of heart, she would get first dibs on being his wife. Ann laughed, "Mr. Neal Newman is that a lop-sided proposal?"

He embraced Ann and kissed her on the forehead and headed to the airport. They had an understanding. For the next five years, their careers would come first.

Neal smiled as he got into the taxi to head to the airport. Ann was intriguing. He understood why Addison couldn't stop talking about her. She always had an answer for effectively dealing with a problem.

As Neal was on his way to the airport, he thought about how Ann said she did not want a traditional wedding. This reminded him of the different cultural traditions he had experienced, and the marriage rituals of the various countries he'd visited. In some traditions, the groom never saw the bride until after the marriage ceremony. In some cultures, the father stood in for the bride at the wedding ceremony, and the groom only saw his bride for the first time in the wedding bed. He knew in the back of his mind that one day he would marry Ann.

After Ann left Hong Kong, she made it a point to find out who Neal Newman was. She already knew how his family name came into existence and that the Newman's were originally from Britain.

The investigator's report regarding the relationship between Addison and Neal concerned her Ann. Neal was in Addison's good graces because he needed an intelligent, younger man who he could mold into his image and likeness. So far, that idea hadn't gone so well. Neal had pushed back on Addison's demands on his time, and his insistence on knowing his every move.

Neal loved to ski and he sometimes disappeared to the slopes to be alone. As usual, Addison was making everything about him and how good he had been at skiing. The investigation revealed something she found extremely concerning. The report revealed that Neal had been hospitalized while on a trip with Addison. It was a known fact Addison used recreational drugs, but the report was inconclusive about whether Neal had taken an over dose of oxycodone, or if the drug had been given to him.

She told Neal that she had conducted the investigation. He was only shocked that she did this after only a month. It made him realize this woman was serious, and she was wasting no time in determining if he would be husband and father material. That night in Hong Kong she told him she wanted three children. Neal couldn't suppress a grin at the thought of Ann Northrop being pregnant with his child.

Six months before the wedding, Ann thought it was time to formally meet Neal's family. Ann had casually spoken to them at social gatherings at Addison's home and company functions. She arranged a dinner party for his parents, his two siblings and sister-in-law. She excluded the children from the dinner party, because of what the family needed to discuss. This decision had nothing to do with Neal's niece and nephews. It was about his brother John because he was not fond of Ann. He had not gotten over his resentment that she would not do the merger for his company.

Neal's sister, Nora, was considering marrying for the third time. She could care less about what anyone else was doing. Her children were in boarding school, and their father was a Texas Oilman. Therefore, it wasn't the money she needed; she was looking for love. How would it be possible for someone to love her, when Nora couldn't love herself? She only had love for the pills and alcohol, and she refused to get help.

Ann had no empathy for people who deliberately abused themselves with drugs or alcohol, especially when they did it in order to punish others. Nora blamed the world for her pain and the failure of two marriages. The parenting of her children had been done by others. She could not accept the fact that she was spoiled, privileged, selfish, and a conceited human being. No one had the guts to tell Nora what an ugly person she was. Nora used her drunken tirades as an excuse to speak her truth. Her parents and her brothers could not stand her vicious drunken tongue. They had learned whenever possible to have the staff ease her out quietly to keep her from causing a scene.

Neal's parents had made their contribution to society and they were ready to depart the stage called life. They had given their children every opportunity their money could afford.

Neal's parent had become Christians six months before his wedding, and their children including Neal weren't happy about their conversion. Neal had no idea of what kind of impact his parent's conversions would have in his life years later.

Chapter Ten: He Shall Live & Not Die

Neal and Ann had been married 15 years and Neal couldn't say they had been happy, thanks to the shenanigans of Addison Chandler. The best thing to have happened to him and Ann were their three sons. Ann was a wonderful mother and the children helped to limit their arguments, since she refused to fight in front of the children.

One of their main battles was over Neal's refusal to leave Addison's company. He reminded Ann of how much she enjoyed the taste of power while working for Addison. Neal wasn't ready to give it up.

Neal was still Senior Vice President of Marketing; after 15 years, he had been with the firm and Addison for over 20 years. Neal knew he didn't want to leave, because of his pride and there were too many perks and fringe benefits that went along with being a part of Addison's inner-circle.

Neal had been blind and now could see that Addison was not going to keep his promise to one day retire and turn the company over to him as President. How could he have been so gullible, especially after Ann kept telling him, this was another one of Addison's narcissistic control games? Addison knew how desperate Neal wanted to be president of the company. Addison dangled the job of president before Neal, because he knew Neal didn't have the strength and the discipline to walk away as his wife had done. Neal and Ann had enough capital to start their own company; but Neal wasn't willing to start from the bottom. After so many years, he felt betrayed, but Addison hadn't betrayed Neal, he had betrayed himself by believing a lie.

Although Neal knew he would never be President of the company, he knew he was still a big player. Over the years when Addison had to be admitted to the psychiatric ward for treatment Neal filled his shoes without question. This was the power he wasn't ready to relinquish.

Addison had told the partners he would step down when he turned seventy-five, and he would then place the company into the hands of Neal. Addison

would soon be turning 80 years old, and he was still as

strong as he was at the age of sixty.

Neal couldn't believe he had gotten himself

involved in Addison Chandler's crazy world. He was

doing things he promised himself he would never do,

and he was not conducting himself like a married man.

His morals had gone out the window.

It was now July 4th 2008, and Neal's madness had

gotten out of control. Neal Newman was ready to

commit suicide. He decided he had cheated on his wife

for the last time. He had popped his last pill, smoked his

last joint and drank his last bottle of Cognac. He felt like

an empty shell of a man, completely devoid of morals.

He had convinced himself he didn't need morals, but he

could no longer pretend. He had become a salve to

Addison, and now he had become his clone. The

recording was stuck in his head and it kept playing over

and over. Neal could hear Ann's words warning him,

"Addison is a monster and wants everyone else to be just like him."

Neal ordered the service of an escort for the evening and shortly afterward a beautiful young girl entered his room. He knew she would soon be lying in his bed, looking into her eyes, he realized she could be his daughter, and she was somebody's daughter. He would be taking her to bed as a temporary fix. What kind of low life pig was he? He had been prepared to take advantage of her youth and innocence; he knew she was innocent because he paid a fortune to take her virginity. He wondered why no one cared enough to protect her and share how precious she would be to someone one day.

The young escort's virginity was being sold to the highest bidder. She had been lied to and manipulated to believe that the money she was making would one day pay for her education in the United States. She looked forward to getting her citizenship and one day being able to send money to help her parents back in Russia.

Someone was getting rich off of pimping her out to the highest bidder, and once they were done using her youth and beauty, they would throw her in the trash like a rag doll.

Addison knew the future was bleak for her, and she might even get involved in drugs to numb her pain. Usually these girls are young and naïve and believe what they are told? They are promised the good life and are told they can land a rich husband, using their feminine assets, and that they will be well cared for. Girls like her are young and naïve, and they don't know that once they are labeled a call girl, that label will stick with them for life. There will those who will never let them forget it. This girl was young and innocent and had no idea how to make love to a man. She probably didn't even have the tools to succeed at life. "How had this misguided young lady found her way into my hotel room?" Addison thought. I am a total stranger, and she hasn't even asked my name.

Neal believed this would be the last day of his life, and if the Christian's were right, he was destined for eternal darkness. He was so disgusted with himself, when he looked in the mirror. Neal threw water on his face, and glanced at the image staring back at him, but he became frightened when he couldn't see the image staring back at him. "Wait, was he going blind?" He called out to the young girl lying on the bed. He didn't even know her name, and there was no response to his cries for help. He threw water on his face a third time. Maybe he was hallucinating. Neal moved carefully with his hands out in front of him. He made his way over to the bed and felt around for the young girl, but she was not there. He swore and cursed till he could no longer find words.

Had the unnamed girl put something in his Cognac? That made no sense, these girls were the top of the line call girls; they could name their price, there was no need to resort to crazy antics. Neal heard a deep guttural voice; "You said you wanted to die." The voice groaned. He stumbled and fell to the floor."

Who was in the room with him? He called out in fear, "Who are you, and what do you want? Why are you in my room?" Neal started crawling on his hands and knees. As he made his way across the room, he saw his life flashing before his eyes. Neal was dismayed at the life he had lived and the people he had hurt. He felt a stabbing pain in his heart. His mind swirled at the thought of not being there for his sons. A vision of his wife and sons praying for him flashed before his eyes. Neal screamed in agony, holding his head, is this what it felt like to lose your mind? Had he gone mad? He couldn't stop the room from spinning. This seemed like a never-ending nightmare. He began to shake uncontrollably, as if he was having a stroke. His arms and legs went numb, and he couldn't speak. Neal had no idea of what was happening to him. Then suddenly, everything stopped.

When Neal opened his eyes he was in a hospital room and there were several doctors surrounding his bed. He could see his wife out of the corner of his eye. His sons were staring blankly through the ICU widow. He wasn't dead after all. He was alive but, his mind was foggy.

When he opened his eyes, the doctor's began asking him all kinds of questions. "Do you know your name? What day is it, and do you know where you are? Mr. Newman, Do you feel any pain? Neal couldn't speak and he still had no feeling in his body. He could understand what they were saying, but he couldn't respond.

Ann ran to his bed. "Oh Neal, I thought you were gone. The doctor's said you wouldn't make it through the night." Me and the boys have been here all night, praying for your recovery. Neal felt sad; he didn't know his wife had been praying for him. He wondered if she'd been going to church too. How could he have known? He was always on the golf course on Sunday's.

Ann whispered softly, "Neal it's okay. I know everything, and I forgive you. I love you and only want you to get well and come home. Neal we're both guilty of turning away, instead of turning towards one another. I wasn't there to support you, when I saw you didn't have the strength to leave the firm."

Ann continued, "I should have encouraged you to start your own company, but instead I became angry and resentful. Neal, I hope you will forgive me. I realize you couldn't help yourself, and I am guilty of the same thing. Neal, we need each other and the only way we're going to get through this catastrophe is to lean on one another.

The room went black again and the ventilator monitors started beeping. The doctors came rushing back into the room. The nurse gave Ann a gentle nudge and led her out of the room. She didn't want to leave Neal's side. In a gentle voice she said "Mrs. Newman, you've done all you can do, you have to trust the doctors to do what's best. The rest is in God's hands."

Ann fell to her knees and cried, "Lord there's nothing more I can do. I trust you completely, and I give Neal totally to you and I leave him in your loving arms. Lord please save my husband."

The next seven days were extreme mental anguish for Neal's family, since they didn't know if he would live or die. The boys wanted to stay at the hospital by their mother's side, Ann didn't force the issue. If she sent them away now and Neal died, she could never forgive herself.

Neal's family arrived from New York. His older brother, John, came with his attorney under the pretense of handling Neal's business interests. This made Ann angry; John was interfering with what Ann was doing on behalf of her husband.

John wanted to discuss funeral arrangements with Ann, which was the furthest thing from her mind. John kept telling her that Neal's condition was hopeless. He insisted, "He's not going to pull through. He is incurable."

Ann reminded John that Neal was not dead yet, and she was sure he was not going to die. John felt his skin crawl every time Ann said, "Neal's not going to die." Despite the doctor's consultation with his family insisting that Neal should be taken off the ventilator, Ann refused and insisted that he would make a full recovery. The doctors explained that Neal was unable to breathe on his own. The machine was keeping Neal alive and breathing for him.

Ann blurted out, "God's going to heal Neal." John told her to stop being foolish. "Even if this God did have the power to heal, Neal doesn't even believe in God, and neither do you." He insisted. "When did you start talking about God?" He questioned.

"Ann the doctors told you to take Neal off the ventilator. If you don't agree to take him off the breathing machine, I'll get a court order against you, and I'll make sure they declare you unfit to be his medical power of attorney." Ann stared John in the face, and pointed her finger at him, "John Martin Newman, God is going to heal Neal; He will live and not die! I'll fight you with every dollar I have to keep Neal alive, until God heals his body, mind and soul, do you understand me?" She said in a menacing tone.

The tone of Ann's voice made John fear her. Especially, when she said his full name and pointed her finger. John felt as if he were in danger. He had never seen this side of Ann. She was always calm and in control, but now it seemed as if fire was exuding from her very being. John couldn't respond, all he could manage to squeak out was, "Call me when he dies, I'm leaving in the morning." Ann told him to leave immediately, and she would have her driver take him to the airport. She asked the others in the room, if any of them wanted to leave with him.

Ann needed family to stand with her in agreement that Neal would be okay. She couldn't allow their unbelief to stop the work that God would do in Neal's life. She imagined that when Neal came through this ordeal, he would be a better man than before he tried to take his life. Ann didn't try to hide the fact that Neal tried to kill himself. While she was praying for Neal, God revealed to her that He had intervened when Neal tried to end his life. God reassured Ann that Neal would live and not die, and that was enough for her.

Chapter Eleven: The Miracle

Ann knew about Neal's infidelity. She didn't share her salvation story and conversion to Christianity with Neal. Her friend, Susan Whitmore, took her to a home bible study in Beverly Hills. She knew some of the women in attendance, because they were involved in the same social circles.

Ann thought this interaction could create new relationships for her, and she could finally be valued by these women of influence. She had no idea that a drastic change was about to happen in her life. How could she know she was about to have her own Damascus Road experience?

When Ann came in the room, she felt a presence, which she later learned was the Spirit of God. She didn't know anything about the Holy Spirit or His anointing power to change her life. Ann felt like she was being bathed in sunlight, as her hand touched the hostesses hand. She felt lightning shoot through her body. Ann was unprepared and embarrassed by what happened next. She stumbled backward and was caught before she fell. A couple of women in the group led her to a seat and handed her a glass of water. She took a few sips of the water and slowly regained her composure.

Ann smelled the scent of incense burning. It was an aroma she had never experienced before. The scent was something you would find in a garden of fresh roses. It was intoxicating and inviting. Elizabeth, the hostess, who had tried to introduce herself earlier, was headed Ann's way again. Ann was embarrassed; her face was flushed red. "Hi, I'm Elizabeth, it's a pleasure to have you." She warmly reassured Ann that there was no need to be embarrassed, since unbeknownst to Ann, the women had been fasting and praying for her and her family for weeks. Ann was grateful for the prayers, and glad that the Lord was answering their prayers.

"Ann, we meet weekly for one hour for bible study. We have a Saturday evening service, where we allow the Holy Spirit to guide our teaching. You're free to leave whenever."

Ann did not notice that the other women had left the room. Elizabeth asked Ann if she could pray with her. Ann had never prayed before, and had no idea of how she should answer.

On the drive home, Ann asked Susan why she hadn't told her about the Lord or taken her to Bible study before now? "I thought we were friends." Ann explained.

"We are friends, Ann. I didn't bring you to Bible study or tell you about God, because of what you told Rita Johnson when she told you she had received Jesus Christ as her personal savior." Ann's face turned blood red.

"There's your answers Ann. It was Rita Johnson who took me to Elizabeth's home and I have been going for the last four years, while still being your friend and praying for you and your family."

Susan went on to explain, "Ann, when I had my nervous breakdown, you and everyone else except for Rita, all stopped coming around. I heard all the jokes behind my back about Susan the snail and Susan so frail. Ann, never once did you take the time to see if I needed a friend. Yes, you sent flowers and a card and every now and then, you even sent someone over to cook for me, but you never came yourself. In the book of John Chapter 15 verse 13, it says, 'Greater love hath no man than this, that he lay down his life for his friends.'"

Ann listened quietly, as Susan continued, "I'm not blaming you. I'm just explaining why I didn't tell you. I had to get well myself, and it was Jesus and the Word of God that made me the woman I am today, and that is a person who loves you enough to want to see you free from pain, hurt and the darkness of this life. I love you enough to tell you that the wages of sin is death. I was wrong to not tell you about God. Will you forgive me? Because of God, I'm stronger today than I was before."

Susan stopped talking for a second to take a breath, then continued. "Ann, I can't promise you that all of your problems will disappear, but I can promise that you will find peace. I cannot promise that your children or your husband will get saved, or even accept the new you. I can't promise that your life will get better; but I can promise that if you were to die tonight that you will be with the Father in Heaven. I can guarantee this to anyone who accepts Jesus Christ as their Lord and Savior." Tears welled up in Ann's eyes. She hadn't said a word for at least 15 minutes.

"I'm sorry for talking so much Ann." Susan apologized. "I can go on for hours about the goodness of Jesus. Do you have any questions?"

Ann finally had a chance to respond, "Yes, I do. How do I ask Jesus Christ into my life?"

Ann jumped as the nurse touched her shoulder, she looked up to hear Neal's nurse telling her the doctor's wanted to talk to her. "Has he awakened?" She asked.

"Mrs. Newman, the doctors will explain everything to you." All kinds of thoughts raced through Ann's mind. Neal's nurse didn't seem anxious, but she wondered if Neal had died. Surely, if Neal was dead she would have sensed an urgency in the nurses voice.

"No, that can't be the case," Ann thought. God had assured her Neal wasn't going to die. Was he paralyzed or did he have another stroke? She had to stop having these negative thoughts. She dared not allow the enemy to play with her mind. "A double-minded man received nothing from the Lord," she thought.

Ann walked slowly down the hall, as she recited the Lord's Prayer. She could only remember the beginning, so her mind shifted to another familiar passage in the Bible.

"The Lord is my Shepherd, I shall not want. He leads me besides the still waters and restores my soul. Yea though I walk through the shadow of death. I will fear no evil." She had that uneasy feeling again, and reciting the 23rd Psalm wasn't helping. Was Neal dying? Was she marching towards the room where his spirit was no longer present?" When she walked into Neal's room, there he was sitting up in bed looking as though nothing had happened.

Neal smiled and stretched his arms towards Ann. She couldn't believe her eyes. She could see from the looks on the doctors faces that they couldn't believe it either? Neal took Ann into his arms and kissed her for the first time in a long time. It wasn't his usual emotionally disconnected peck on the cheek, and Ann didn't pull away even though he had morning breath. She asked the nurse if she could her get her husband some mouth wash. Neal was healed, and it was nothing short of a miracle!

The buzzards had started swarming again. Of course Addison attributed Neal's miraculous healing to all the specialists he had flown in from all over the country. Addison provided the doctors with housing and anything they needed to get Neal back on his feet.

Addison had managed to squash all of the rumors regarding Neal's suicide attempt. He told Neal's colleagues that he was suffering from exhaustion from working too hard. Addison wouldn't allow anyone to visit Neal in the hospital. Only Neal's immediate family was allowed to visit. To make sure his wishes were carried out, Addison hired a twenty-four hour security service. The security service had a list of who could and could not see Neal. Ann protested, when she couldn't even get her friend Susan in to see Neal. Addison's security team was instructed not to let any of Ann's friends on Neal's floor. Addison made sure Neal had a room on a secure floor, reserved for the rich and famous.

Addison went as far as having Neal's medical records sealed. He was taking no chances of anything being leaked to the media. The doctors were not permitted to put any of Neal's medical history into hospital computers. Addison knew all too well about hackers and how easy it was to get information in the 21th century.

Addison also brought in special coding and recording equipment for Neal's doctors. These devices were used whenever Addison had to be hospitalized. The doctors used the equipment to communicate with one another. They also used special recording devices to keep track of Neal's medical records. The telephone lines weren't secure enough for Addison. He had done enough spying to know all of the potential vulnerabilities and the extent of what could be found once those systems were cracked.

Addison's security technology made the FBI electronic communications look like child's play. He knew that far too much hacking still goes on in our Federal government, and this was a source of contention for Addison. Addison couldn't understand why the US government still used digital communications, for the life of him.

Addison learned years ago that once financial transactions and personal records were transmitted over the airways, the information was no longer safe. He had lobbied for the federal government to stop using wire and electronic transfers.

Addison's company had invested in clone carriers. These carriers were new and no one truly knew what they were, they looked human, but they weren't, and they weren't robots either. This was new underground technology, that had never been revealed to the public. It was still top secret, or so our government thought. They were able to do whatever Addison needed done, from security to transferring money or equipment.

Before Ann could pull herself out of Neal's arms, Addison walked in. They must have called him before they sent for her to come to her husband's room. Addison brushed by Ann, as those he didn't see her. He grabbed Neal's arm and said, "Welcome back, old boy. I thought you were a goner." Ann interrupted him. "I told you Neal was not going to die, Addison." Addison turned and looked Ann in the face, with the most sinister look, as if to say, "Shut your ugly mouth."

Ann could feel the hatred that welled up in his heart and mind. She knew Addison wanted her to disappear. He laughed again, in his sinister tone.

"Yes, Ann I've been hearing about your prayer meetings and your continual prayers for Neal's healing and recovery. But, Neal's recovery has nothing to do with any miracle you prayed for. Neal has the best doctors' money could buy. They came because I called."

Ann's face felt warm and flushed. "Believe what you want, Addison. I know who healed my husband. If your high powered doctors weren't afraid to tell you the truth, they would tell you the same thing. They had nothing to do with Neal's healing. All they did was pump fluids into his body to keep him hydrated, and you call that top-notch medicine Addison? Addison I don't care what you think of me, you can't ignore the fact that my husband was healed by the supernatural power of the Holy Spirit!"

Ann continued, "Addison I know you don't believe that there is a God who created the heavens and earth, but He exists. My Savior, Jesus Christ interceded for Neal, and my God, Jehovah healed his body. Ann explained, "Addison it was God that spared your life and the life of your family in Australia. Yes, I've heard how you've been searching for years to find the answers to why you and your family didn't drown that night in Australia. Addison, the same Jesus who healed Neal is the same Jesus that saved your family."

Addison cursed, as he walked out of Neal's room. Neal didn't say a word, but pulled Ann in the bed with him. She was disappointed that Neal didn't say anything to back her up. It was as though he was in agreement with Addison. Ann laid her head on Neal's chest, as tears flowed from her eyes. She prayed for her husband and thanked God for his healing.

Jehovah was able to take care of Addison. That wasn't her job. She had a renewed commitment to her husband and sons. Her prayers had been answered, and she was willing to do everything in her power to strengthen the relationships in her family.

Little did Ann know that Neal had already given his life to Christ, and was a new believer? Ann sensed something in her spirit two days later when they released Neal from the hospital. He was not in a hurry to get back to work. Addison told him to take all the time he needed. Neal told Ann he wanted to take her and the boys on a vacation. This was a shock to her, because she had begged Neal for the last two years to go on vacation with his family, but he was always too busy with work. Neal called his three sons and asked them where they wanted to go. The boys were in utter disbelief. This was not the father they knew. Their father had asked them to go on a vacation in the middle of the school semester and it's wasn't even a business trip. The boys began to shout out all kinds of countries, "Let's go to Paris. No, let's go to India! No, what about Africa?"

Neal turned to Ann, and asked, "Honey, where would you like to go?" The boys laughed, and all jumped in their dad's lap. They had never heard their dad call their mother, Honey.

"Boys, go get packed, while your mother and I figure out where we're going. We're leaving as soon as she comes up with a destination. The jet is already fueled and ready to go." The boys ran to their rooms screaming. Could this be true that they were going on vacation, as a family? It wasn't an arranged business meeting for their father and Addison. The boys couldn't remember ever being this happy. They were always competing with Addison for their father's affection. Whenever Neal promised the boys a camping trip, somehow Addison always seemed to intervene. Neal regretted how he had allowed Addison to keep him from his family.

Ann made her decision. "We're going to Yellowstone National Park." The boys will have a wonderful time hiking and camping. Ann wanted to scream at the top of her lungs, but she maintained her composure. She wanted her family to witness the greatness of God and His creation. She had learned that she shouldn't preach to her family. The Bible taught her that by her chaste behavior, her family could be won over to Christ. Her bible study was teaching her to become a living epistle to be read by those she encountered in her daily life. She learned that everyone was God's precious creation, no matter their race, creed, or the color of their skin. They were all created by God, and when he created man, he said that it was a good thing that He had done. The Bible taught her that God is no respecter of persons, and that we are all created by God. She also understood that we are not all God's children, until we accept his gift of salvation.

According to the Bible, God created all souls in his image and likeness, and He gave us all the free will to choose whether we would believe in God. For Ann, that meant that when we hate someone, we hate the very image of God's likeness. Ann was delighted to know that all people have the opportunity to become the sons and daughters of the Most High God. Her heart was filled with joy in knowing that only God could have ordained this day for her and her family to be going on vacation. It was the end of April. This was living proof that there was a God. Neal even allowed her to decide where the family would go. The boys were overwhelmed with excitement.

"Mom, we don't know what to pack. We have no idea of where we're going."

"How does Yellowstone National Park sound?" Ann yelled.

The children screamed and hugged one another, at the thought of spending a vacation in Yellowstone. Neal kissed Ann again. The boys teased, "Daddy loves mommy!"

"Wow, two kisses in the same week." I must have died and gone to heaven, or this is an awfully good dream, that I don't want to wake up from."

Neal told the boys not to worry about packing and that they would buy everything they need once they landed in Wyoming. Neal asked his sons if they could tell him which states Yellowstone National Park was located? Jackson, the youngest of the three boys said, "I don't know."

Thomas, the second oldest said, "The park is in Wyoming and Idaho."

Benjamin, the oldest said, "Sorry brother's, you're both wrong. Yellowstone is located in Wyoming, Idaho and Montana."

"You're right," Neal said. "The park is located in three states, and we're going to all three!"

Ann responded, "Let's get out of here before your dad changes his mind." They all raced to the car.

This was the happiest Ann had seen her family in years, and her heart was flowing with thanksgiving. The Bible study group had taught Ann that she could pray anytime and in any place. There was no limited to what she could ask the Lord. Her study group taught her that God loves to shower his children with good things, and enlighten their minds with truth. They said that once someone's mind is open to the truth and we put God first in our lives, material things lose their importance.

As Neal backed out of the drive way, Ann prayed for a safe and enjoyable vacation for her family. She hoped that her family would experience the wonderment of God's creation in Yellowstone National Park.

Chapter Twelve: Ann, A Pillar of Strength

Just as Ann had not shared her salvation story with Neal, he had also been keeping a secret from Ann. It was not yet time for true confession. Now, it was time for Neal to enjoy his family for a much needed vacation. Neal wanted to become a better husband and father. He could tell Ann wanted to talk about what she had been through the past couple of weeks, but Neal was still in awe of his miraculous recovery. He heard every word Ann had spoken, while he was in a coma. He wasn't ready to talk about it though. He admired the way that Ann was so open and willing to share her testimony and her love for Jesus, but he didn't have the courage to share his faith with Ann. Not yet, anyway.

Neal invited Christ into his heart, before everything went black in his hotel room. He loved the joy he saw in Ann, now that she had developed a relationship with Jesus. Her happiness was obvious in the way she carried herself; Neal found it amazing that she was so transformed. Ann was a new person; she had started being more kind, loving, patient, and caring with the boys. And, she seemed to have a deeper understanding of his needs. She didn't force him to speak about his near death experience, nor did she try to push her religion on him. The closest she came to that was the day at the hospital, when she told Addison who had healed him, and that it was the same God who had saved him and his family in Australia.

Addison didn't question Neal about his attempted suicide. He dismissed unpleasant situations that he didn't want to deal with by simply ignoring them. That was fine with Neal, since he wasn't ready to explain anything to Addison. Neal realized that the truth would come out soon enough, especially when he announced to Addision that he planned to leave the company. He would also have to come clean with his wife about his double life; although he knew she had her suspicions.

Neal's thoughts were jumping from one thing to another. He was overwhelmed with thoughts of what he would tell Ann, once their vacation was over. Neal knew his confession would probably destroy what was left their marriage. The marriage had been on life support for the last couple of years, and Neal had no idea about Ann's new found faith in Jesus. He doubted that her new relationship with God would be enough to bring healing and forgiveness after his big confession. He wasn't sure she would be able to find it in her heart to forgive him for what he had to tell her about his extramarital affairs.

The person in the car next to him blew his horn; Neal was drifting into the next lane. Benjamin yelled, "Watch out dad! You almost hit that car!" Ann remained silent. Neal experienced severe trauma, and was coping the best he knew how. She knew from the look on his face that he was in deep thought. He needed to forgive himself.

Neal apologized, "Sorry guys I wasn't paying attention." The rest of the drive to the airport went smoothly, and without incident. The drive seemed extremely long to Ann. The traffic was normal, considering it was the middle of the week. The excitement of being able to get-away with the family made the drive seem longer.

Ann wanted her family unified more than anything else, she felt a sense of peace just knowing that their entire family was taking this trip. The look on the boys faces told the whole story. They were ecstatic to be with both of their parents. They had gotten used to their mother taking them to their practices and games. They stopped searching the stands for their father's face a long time ago. Ann always made excuses for Neal's absence, but the kids weren't fooled. Their father was a deadbeat, and no matter how many different excuses she conjured up, it didn't change that fact.

Ann reminisced about how she had fallen in love with Neal, as she rode through the traffic. She wanted nothing more than to be with her husband and sons. She hadn't thought about it in a while, but their marriage hadn't always been strained. Addison had played a part in driving a wedge between them. He didn't like seeing people happy, especially her and Neal. Ann had allowed her guard to be down once she no longer worked for Addison. She was so overjoyed to be pregnant with their first child that she gave no more energy to Addison's mind games. Ann was preparing for the birth of their son, and being a mother was all that mattered to her.

Neal went to every doctor's appointment with Ann, even accompanying her to Lamaze classes. Some of the women in the class told them they were going to be great parents.

During a meeting with Addison and his secretary, Neal informed them of Ann's due date. He wanted to make it clear to them that no matter what was happening at the office, or with the business on that day, he would be at the hospital for his son's birth. That was the start of trouble with Addison, who had never attended the birth of any of his children.

Addison chimed in as if he was the authority on having children. He proclaimed forcefully, "Neal you'll be wasting your time sitting around waiting for your son to be born. This is Ann's first child, you could be there two days." Neal laughed, "Addison, you know Ann, and that's not about to happen." Neal's statement didn't stop Addison from trying to plan an overnight business trip for him and Neal. Addison assured Neal he would be back in plenty of time for the birth of his son. Neal chuckled, "Addison, you're kidding me! I'm not leaving Ann. You'll have to send one of your other clones." Neal knew the remaining five partners would be excited about the opportunity to step into his shoes.

Ann was ecstatic; she couldn't believe Neal put in a request for family leave. Neal stood his ground with Addison. He insisted that he was going to be there for his son's birth. Addison was determined to make sure that would be the first and last birth Neal would be attend.

Ann wasn't wasting precious time on Addison or his childish games. Their son, Benjamin's birth was the greatest miracle she had ever experienced. This tiny infant was beautiful, and she had instantly fallen in love with her son. From then on, her every waking thought was concern for his care.

Benjamin continued to be Ann's world as Neal slipped further and further away. As years passed, and their other two sons were born, she and Neal grew more distant. Let him have his travel and the business world. She had her sons. Ann couldn't remember exactly when she stopped caring about what her husband did. She had allowed time and Addison's company to separate her from what she truly wanted in life, besides her sons, and that was a healthy marriage.

Neal's drinking and staying away from home had become more frequent, and if he wasn't upset with Ann, he was furious with Addison or about what was going on at the office. He was battling with himself over something he couldn't control, because Addison was in control. The very things Neal swore he wouldn't allow to happen to him happened. He lost his family, thanks in part to Addison. Addison kept demanding more and more of the time he should have been spending with his family. The business trips got longer, and his sons' grew older without him in their lives. He was like a weekend visitor to his sons. Neal watched Ann's love for him grow cold, as she turned all of her affection to her children. In the past, Ann would stay up late to wait for Neal to get home and tell him what the children had done during the day. She even kept a weekly video diary of the children for Neal to watch, until she noticed that he started losing interest, and taking more business trips that kept him away from home for longer periods of time.

Ann and Neal started avoiding one another and their relationship began to suffer. Neal started spending nights at the country club instead of coming home after late business meetings. Ann found hotel receipts in his suit jacket when she sent out his dry cleaning. That's when Ann knew Neal was seeing other women. She was not about to let Neal's escapades break up her son's home, even though he had been absent and had not participated in his son's lives the way she wanted him to. When it was important to the boys that Neal attend a school event or an awards ceremony, he showed up.

After years of fighting with Neal, Ann didn't understand the power Addison wielded over his employees, especially her husband. Neal and Ann had enough money to start their own company, but Neal didn't want to, and this baffled Ann. She was even willing work with Neal to make sure he succeeded. She knew she could be a tremendous asset to their company, but Neal could not tear himself away from Addison.

Ann was sure that Addison was a Satanist; no one could be that evil without working black magic. Addison insisted that he didn't believe in the occult, but his actions seemed to say otherwise. Money is a powerful tool that can enslave people and gain their loyalty, but to see men turn their backs on their families was mind boggling to Ann. She had seen Addison destroy families when she worked for him. She wasn't concerned at the time, because she didn't have a family, and never imagined in her wildest dreams that it could happen to her.

Neal never betrayed Addison by sharing with Ann what went on after the secret partner meetings. He knew Addison dabbled in the occult. Neal was privy to the fact that Addison entertained those who practiced "white magic." They called themselves practitioners. They use their supernatural powers to speak blessings over the company and employees. Neal believed the practitioners were using spells and supernatural power over the partners in the boardroom. Neal, and the rest of the partners, were doing things they would have never dream of doing to themselves or family without this supernatural intervention.

Ann, and the other wives were aware of the escort services Addison set up for their husbands when they went on business trips. A few couples in the company had gotten divorced over their husband's infidelity. The majority of the men did not outwardly object to Addison's entertainment for their trips; if they did, he simply excluded them from upcoming business trips. Being excluded costed them millions. They didn't realize it wasn't Addison who had made them filthy rich; it was their own hard work and dedication to the firm that gained them wealth. Addison owned the company, but the partners paid their dues with blood, sweat and tears. They dreaded a potential call from Addison's office that could turn their world upside down. Neal, and the six partners, who were part of Addison's inner circle, endured Addison's sick games on a regular basis.

Ann felt sick to her stomach as she realized she had also played Addison's game; by turning a blind eye to what she knew her husband was doing. This was going to be a difficult test for both of them. Ann wondered if they would be able to face the truth, truly forgive one another, and bury the past.

Ann heard the familiar sound of the engine, and could see the jet off in the distance. She knew the sound of Addison's jet from the times she would have to drop

Neal off, with a last minute call for a business meeting. Addison's personal pilot was waiting for them, as they pulled into the private hanger. Jake, the pilot, let Neal know he was on standby, waiting for his family to arrive. "Where to Mr. Newman?" Jake asked. Addison probably sent Jake to keep an eye on Neal. Ann could care less. She was with her family, and they were boarding a private jet. Addison had already instructed his pilot to check the logs to see what Neal had previously ordered for his trips He wanted to make sure that everything Neal's family could imagine was on board. Neal hadn't informed Addison of his intended destination, so Addison sent his jet with the intent of impressing the boys. Over the years, Ann had limited her son's contact with Addison as much as possible. She had made up her mind that if Neal wasn't strong enough to leave the firm, she would avoid as many social events as possible with Addison. Ann refused to allow Addison to have influence over her sons the way he did with Neal.

Jake announced over the intercom, "Please fasten your seatbelts. We're off to Yellowstone National Park." The boys threw up the Victory sign. As far as Ann was concerned, it was the exact right sign for the occassion. They did have the Victory, and this vacation proved it.

Jake came over the intercom again and announced, "Sit back and relax. Once the aircraft hits thirty-thousand feet you'll be free to take off your seatbelts and move about the cabin, watch movies or do whatever makes you happy. Mr. and Mrs. Newman, Mr. Addison has a bottle of champagne chilling for the two of you. The fight should be no longer then 95 minutes and we'll touchdown with mild 70 degree weather."

Neal squeezed Ann's hand slightly, as if to say thank you. He wondered what was on Ann's mind, and why she had been so quiet on the drive to the airport. There was a lot on both of their minds. Neal took a deep breath and held Ann's hand up to his lips and willed her to stop him from the words he knew would to break her heart. Neal had been living a double life for the past two years, and he knew Ann had no idea. He wondered if Ann would still trust God to fix their relationship. Ann had been so happy the last several weeks.

Neal was praying that Ann would find the same strength to stand up for their marriage that she had shown his brother, John, and Addison. She had won the battle to save his life by keeping him on life support. John and Addison had given up and believed the doctor's report that there was no hope he would recover. Ann told Neal she was willing to spend every dollar to fight Addison and John in court, if she had to. Neal knew from the day he met Ann she was a fighter. She had stepped into the male dominated field of finance, and made her name known around the world. She stood up to Addison when no one else had the tenacity to stand their ground, and she never flinched when the fiery darts were thrown. Although it had been many years Ann's name was still mentioned in board rooms around the world. Ann had single handedly taken the brokerage firm global.

Since Neal's hospitalization, he had asked himself if he was jealous of his wife's previous success. He knew he had resented her for having the strength to leave the firm and leave him behind. He had wanted Ann to start a company with him of their own. He thought it made him seem weak, because it was her suggestion, and not his. Now it seemed foolish, and he wondered if he'd been drinking at the time she suggested it.

Neal's heart raced again, at the thought that once the vacation was over, he would have to make his confession. He knew this might be the last vacation he would be taking with his family, and the end of his marriage. All he could do was count on the grace he had been given when his body was miraculously healed. Neal had experienced several unusual occurrences in the past few weeks. If you told him these things would take place a month ago, he would have never believed it.

Neal was continually praying that the new found faith Ann had in Jesus would be enough to sustain her, when she learned that he was a cheat.

Neal had no way of knowing if Ann would be leaving Yellowstone as his wife, or staying behind with his sons. He knew whatever the consequences, he brought this pain upon himself. The harder he tried to push the thoughts away, the more he noticed the hope in Ann's eyes. Neal knew she was praying this would be a new beginning for them. He was determined to enjoy his family and prayed that all would work itself out.

Chapter Thirteen: Too Old to Have a Baby

Ann was holding Neal's hand as she drifted off to sleep. She thought about how much she missed her parents and wished they had not waited so long to have her. Ann knew her parents would love Neal and their grandchildren. She remembered what her father said about staying true for that special one. Ann realized as she drifted off to sleep that Neal was that special one. She had forgotten how special Neal was to her, and in her sleep she felt Neal lean over and kiss her forehead. Ann heard the boys say, "Not again!" And let out a hearty laugh. She didn't wake to the boy's laughter.

Her sleep was taking her deeper into her past. She was dreaming about the fact that she was an only child, and she had always resented her parents for not having more children. In Hong Kong, Neal and Ann had discussed that he didn't want children, but he knew for his corporate image a child added to his credibility of being a stable man. One child would have been fine with Neal, but no way was Ann stopping with one child.

Ann was being haunted in her sleep by the memory of being an only child. She would settle for two children, but never only one. She had excelled in her studies to prevent loneliness. Ann had her share of invisible playmates and at times didn't know what was imaginary or real. As a child, Ann knew nothing about supernatural beings. Her parents often found her talking to her invisible friends. They thought it was cute. She had special names for her playmates. Her mother always told her encouraged her whenever she'd emote about being an only child, "Ann, you're special. Children are given to older couples as special gifts, and one day you'll make a difference in this world, you wait and see."

Losing both her parents was surreal for Ann. She had no one to turn. Her mother was her in their late forties when she was born. Ann's mother was an only child, so she had no relatives on her mother's side, and her father refused to associate with his brothers. Ann didn't ever know her uncle's names. When her father died, one of his brothers had read his obituary in the Chicago Tribune. It was sad when her Uncle Eric showed up at the funeral home. He didn't know his brother had married and had a daughter. Eric told Ann that when her Uncle James left home for college he never looked back. He disowned his family and the family never heard from him again. Eric remembered James saying he had to get away from the poverty and pain of his past, because if he stayed he would be like his father and walk away from his family when things got difficult. When her Grandma Rose died, they were sure James would return home for her funeral, but he didn't. We never blamed James, he was never satisfied with his plight in life, he always wanted more, and Ann didn't have the heart to tell Eric her father never found his place in life, because he was too scared as a child. He never got over not having not having money or enough to eat. He became so obsessed with saving every penny, that he never enjoyed life. Because of his obsession with money, if he had his way, she would have never been born. Ann was an extra expense, in her father's eyes. She would be taking away from his saving. Once she was born, her father learned to love her. Ann knew she would never see her Uncle Eric again, even though they both agreed to keep in contact. Ann could see from his clothing that they lived in two different worlds.

Ann's mother died first, of a heart attack, and her father died of a broken heart. She was one of the few people he valued more than the almighty dollar.

Ann turned in her sleep as she was being pulled deeper into her dreams. She was thinking about her father and the story he told her about the saddest day of his life. The day he stopped believing in God. He wanted no parts of a God who could allow four little boys to go to bed with their stomachs empty and crying for their father. Her father and his brother's suffered for weeks until a neighbors found his youngest brother Madison on her door step crying, and saying he was hungry. The neighbors brought food to his mother's house and helped her get welfare for the children. Her father couldn't understand why a father would leave four defenseless children, with a woman who couldn't care for herself, much less four young boys. His mother had never worked outside the home, so she lacked skills to find a job. Her father learned while growing up that his mother suffered from deep depression. His father left when he could no longer deal with her mental illness. He was selfish. He couldn't handle his wife's illness either, and he left four little boys to deal with her mental illness alone.

The neighbors helped when they could. Her father said his mother always resented the fact that she never had a little girl. Ann's parents gave her the middle name "Rose", after her paternal grandmother. That was their way of giving her the daughter she never had.

Ann smiled in her sleep and turned and laid her head on Neal's shoulder. She remembered her mother told her that each year she would plant a new rose bush in her garden, because she had no children. Ann wanted a daughter and because she didn't have one. She would give names to the roses. When the roses would bloom she would name the most beautiful rose in the garden Ann, because she always said if she had a daughter her name would be Ann Rose Northrop. Her father's entire life had been consumed with amassing wealth. When she thinks back to the stories her mother shared about how her father would not allow her to have children because he didn't want to spend their money, her heart would break for her mom. She would look at her sons and tears would fill her eyes at the thought of them never having been born.

Ann's mother told her to always make her own money, so that she wouldn't have to depend on her husband. She cautioned her to always tuck a dollar in her apron. Her mother said, "Ann your grandmother called it having "Chicken soup money".

Ann asked her mother "Why was it called chicken soup money?"

Her mother told her "You can have chickens' today and feathers tomorrow."

"Listen Ann, your great grandmother use to say that things can change in a day. She was right. Women have to always be mindful of their vulnerability."

Ann was in a deep restless sleep on Neal's shoulder and kept trying to adjust her head as if that would make the stories stop invading her thoughts. Now she was thinking about her mother's parents. They didn't go to church, but they read the Bible. Her mother told her, "Ann, your grandfather was a hard man. Your grandmother didn't believe in God, because of your grandfather. She would see her husband reading the Bible and preaching out of the it, but he didn't practice what he preached. He wasn't kind or loving to his wife and children." Ann's mother told her that this is why she never took her to church; not that there was anything wrong with church, but because she didn't experience the love her father preached about in the Bible. Her mom didn't want Ann's head filled with foolish stories.

She didn't want Ann to experience the same disappointment in life, or have her depending on a man to dictate whether or not she had children. Ann's mother made sure she had the money for college, and that she was educated to make her own decisions.

Ann's mother told her to make sure she knew what type of man she wanted to marry. Just as her mother's words invaded her dreams, Neal turned to adjust his body in the seat, and Ann was awakened. Her head was pounding, and she could feel the plane descending as it prepared for landing.

Neal asked, "Are you okay Ann? You were thrashing around in your sleep; you couldn't seem to get comfortable on my shoulder. Were you having a bad dream?"

The boys were peering out the window at the mountains, "They're beautiful," they said in unison. "Can we live here?"

Neal's stomach did a somersault at the sound of that statement. Wyoming might wind up being their new home, he thought. Neal didn't want to think about that right now. He had three weeks to hike, camp, go water rafting, stay up late and sit around a campfire with his family.

The pilot had to remind the boys to take their seats and buckle up, but they were too excited to sit still. They wanted to go fishing. "Who said anything about fishing?" Exclaimed their father.

The jet made a smooth landing. As it taxied to the hanger, the boys were out of their seats again. "Safety first." Neal laughed as he corralled them back to their seats.

Ann said, "Neal it's going to be challenging to hold your son's back for the next three weeks. They are rambunctious. You have kind of been out of the loop for a while, and this is their normal pace. You're going to have a great time bonding with them on this trip. Benjamin especially needs time with you, Neal. He's turning into a young man and will be thirteen soon. This is the age were a young man needs his father to tell him about the birds and the bees. They've been missing their father and they want their Daddy back."

As they waited for the limousine to take them to the hotel, she felt sadness invade her spirit, at the thought of not being born and knowing it was her father who had insisted to the doctor that his wife was too old to have a baby. What a beautiful life she would have missed out on if she had never been born. That means these three handsome sons would never have been born either. Ann treasured the gift of life.

Neal noticed that there had been something on her mind, ever since they took off from the airport, but he was allowing her to have her space, as she had done for him. He knew when Ann was ready to share what was troubling her, she would.

On their drive to the hotel, Ann continued to look out the window. As the trees and mountains faded in the background, her thoughts returned to the stories her mother had told her about her birth, and how she was taken by ambulance to the emergency room because she fainted in the grocery store. Her mother had no idea she was pregnant. Her father tried to convince, Dr. Dixon, the emergency room doctor to recommend a procedure to terminate his wife pregnancy, because he was too old to be a father. Her father went as far as to pretend that he fainted, after the doctor announced that his wife was five months pregnant. Her father was fifty years old with white hair, and did not want to be a father at his age. He wanted didn't want anyone to know that he was going to be a father at fifty.

"Ann your father never wanted me to find out it was his idea and not Dr. Dixon's to terminate the pregnancy. He knew I would hate him forever, if I found out. Your father could feel my resentment toward him. He knew I was already upset about having a child at forty eight, and not in my twenties. I was determined not to have cesarean. I delivered you by natural childbirth.

Chapter Fourteen: Paradise Restored

The limousine pulled into the driveway of the hotel, and Ann didn't understand why all these stories were resurfacing now concerning her parents; they had been dead for years. What did the history of her parents and her birth have to do with her now? Granted, she had heard two different stories, but did it really matter whose story was true?

As Neal helped Ann out of the limousine, he reminisced about helping her out of the limousine on their honeymoon, which seemed a life time ago. Ann was still an attractive woman, who believed in healthy diet and exercise. She was the same weight after children as on the day they married; Neal couldn't say the same for himself. Neal had put on about twenty pounds and he knew the extra weight was a result of his drinking, which he did to try to fit in, and where had it gotten him, almost too the brink of disaster, that's where.

Neal wanted Ann to know he was truly remorseful for the past two years. He knew the only way to show her was by his actions. He had neglected his duties as a husband and father. He would not be able to talk his way out of the disaster he made of his shattered life; it affected his son's, just as much as it affected him and Ann. How could he have been so careless and selfish? He was about to shatter four innocent lives. They might hate him and may not be able to forgive him. They would never again see him as their hero and protector.

Ann caressed Neal's arm as the boys grabbed a hold of his jacket, and squealed, "Come on dad, let's get going; we don't have all day." Neal stopped in his tracks and gazed at his three sons in front of him, and exclaimed. "Boys, we have three weeks to enjoy each other; we don't have to do everything the first day". "We're going to dinner and afterward we'll map out our plans for the next three weeks."

Neal continued to explain how their plans would go. "We'll start with your choices for the next two days

Jefferson; your turn will be next, Thomas, and last but not least, Benjamin."

"Each of you will have two days to do whatever you want. We'll do everything together as a family, no one running off alone, understood? I want the three of you to go to the gift shop and pick up pamphlets on what the Park offers at this time of the year, while your mother and I get the keys to the rooms. Benjamin, you're in charge." Jackson mockingly said, "Why is it always Benjamin who gets to be in charge? I'm almost eight; I should get a turn to be in charge."

Benjamin said, "Dad that's okay with me. Let Jackson be in charge, and when we get lost and the bears come out of the woods, remember he's in charge." The whole family had a good laugh. "There are bears?" Jackson asked, his voice quivering, "Maybe I'll wait till I'm nine."

The boys scampered off to the gift shop while their parents walked to the front desk. The concierge smiled as they approached the counter and greeted them with a warm hello, "Here are your keys, Mr. and Mrs. Newman. Everything has been taken care of for your arrival. You have the two adjoining suites and we'll do everything possible to make sure you enjoy your stay. The boys will have their own personal guide, if you'd like, or we can arrange for a family tour of the park. Any morning you desire to sleep in, we can entertain the boys for you." Neal replied, "That will not be necessary, we'll be doing all the activities with the boys and their guide." Neal hadn't been hiking or camping since he was a Boy Scout.

As Neal and Ann turned to walk away from the front desk, the boys returned with both hands filled with pamphlets of activities at Yellowstone National Park. Neal smiled at his son's enthusiasm and asked, "Did you leave any for the other guests?" Thomas grinned sheepishly and said, "I told Jackson not to take so many."

The air was cool in the late afternoon this time of the year in Wyoming. Ann had to remind herself it was

April. She was thankful for the indoor swimming pool; she knew the boys would want to go swimming after dinner. Neal had asked at the front desk where he could take his family shopping. The concierge smiled and said, "Mr. Newman, everything your family needs is in the hotel. Our retail shops are located on the second floor." "If there is anything you need, and we don't have it, we can have it for you by this afternoon or in the morning at the latest."

Ann smiled to herself, thinking these inquiries were showing Neal had not been on a vacation with his family for a few years. They were staying at a five star resort so there was no need to go to the front desk. These arrangements could have been done on his telephone or on the app. Ann didn't mention this to Neal; this was her small way of show Neal that she was prepared to let him take the lead. It felt good to have Neal ask the questions and inquire about what his family wanted to do in order to enjoy their vacation.

After dinner they went to the second floor to shop for clothing and equipment. Neal got a list of what the boy's would need from the guide. The list gave instructions for each season, and since it was early April they would be able to fish, enjoy Old Faithful waterfalls, see wildlife, go to Mammoth Hot Springs, and overnight camping in the Grand Canyon of the Yellowstone, which was all on the boys' lists. Neal was up for everything except skiing. The guides color coded what each boy would need, which gave them the opportunity to pick out their own gear. This made Jackson feel on top of the world, and like he was on an equal plain with his brothers.

Neal strolled over to the swimsuit section for women; he realized he had not seen his wife in a swimsuit for a few years. He was too busy with his own selfish desires to be the husband and father he should have been. Ann eased over to where Neal was holding two beautiful bathing suits in his hand, and she asked "Who are those for?" Neal turned and smiled, "You!"

The feeling of love made her heart; swell and she wanted to fall into his arms and give Neal the most passionate kiss. The only reason she retrained herself was for the sake of the boys who had enough kissing for one day.

Ann was hoping that this would be the night she would find herself in the arms of her husband. She would not turn him away as she had for the past few years. She would gladly receive her husband to her arms once again; she could no longer tell herself she did not miss Neal's warm embrace and gentle touch. She had been the only one hurting, because in her heart, she knew he had turned to another woman. Ann whispered a prayer that it wasn't too late for them to save their marriage. She was filled with regret at the thought that she helped push her husband into the arms of another woman. She was willing to fight to win back her husband's love and respect. Ann felt certain in that moment that nothing was impossible.

Jackson ran to his mother, and yelled, "Mommy look at all this great stuff I have for camping. Now can we go swimming?" Neal interjected, "Yes, of course, let's all go swimming." He looked at Ann and said, "Put this one on." In the room, Neal whispered in Ann's ear, "I hope we'll make it to the swimming pool." Ann felt like a woman being asked out on a first date. Why was she so nervous? After all this was her husband. Neal went across the room to the adjoining door to the boys' room and locked the door. Ann's heart began to race and she thought, "Not now I'm not ready." Neal took Ann in his arms and put his lips on hers. The blood rushed to her head and the room went blank. The only word she could say was, "Neal". Suddenly there was a knock at the door. It was Jackson "Mom why is this door locked? I need to get in." Ann softly said, "I'm coming Jackson." Neal pulled Ann back on the bed, "Let him wait." he moaned Ann was shocked. The boys had to wait, for the first time in their lives.

Neal got up and open the door and asked, "Jackson what do you want with your mother?" Jackson said, "Nothing. I just wanted to know why the door was locked. Mom has never locked her door." Neal turned and looked at Ann and responded you have our sons spoiled. Jackson looked at his father and said, "You don't have on your swimming trunks. Does mom have on her bathing suit?" Neal and Ann laughed. Seeing his parents interact with each other was new for Jackson, who had gotten used to sleeping with his mother while his father was out of town. Ann was thinking things might be changing soon which is what she hoped for.

Neal felt he had won the lottery when his wife walked out of the restroom in her bathing suit. He found himself thinking maybe he didn't want her to wear that suit to the pool. Ann had a beautiful shape even after having three boys. She was always discipline about what she ate and made sure the boys ate healthy as well. Neal knew he must have been a fool to allow another man to take him away from a beautiful woman like this.

His eyes were open now, and he could truly see that Addison was jealous of his and Ann's relationship. Neal had been blind with pride and ambition to see it before. What was he trying to prove during all of those wasted years? This woman had given him everything he needed, yet he had turned his back on her and his sons to be a Salve to Addison. The only thing Ann ever wanted from him was to be a decent husband and a good father to their sons. She had tried over the years to awaken Neal to the pitfalls of Addison's narcissistic behavior, but her words of caution fell on deaf ears, since Neal was drunk with alcohol, and the desire for power.

Neal relaxed once he saw his wife put on a wraparound over her bathing suit. He had his nerve to want to be jealous having her cover up. He thought men are truly chauvinistic wanting modesty for their woman while taking advantage of everyone else. Neal knew if his wife was willing to forgive him after his confession he'd be faithful to her the rest of his life. He wanted the chance to cherish again what he had all along. Suddenly,

Neal knew he wouldn't be returning to work for Addison. It was clear to him that even if Ann refused to give their marriage another chance, he was done with Addison forever.

Neal and Ann glanced at each other and said at the same time, "You have been doing a lot of thinking." They both laughed as they stepped into the elevator. Thomas said, "Mommy please don't kiss Dad at the pool." Neal laughed," Is it embarrassing, son?" "Not really," Thomas said, "I'm just not used to the two of you kissing." Benjamin looked embarrassed and said "Me neither." The water was refreshing, and the boys enjoyed splashing water on their dad. Ann realized that Neal was a good man who had lost his way. Her faith was teaching her that everyone deserved a second chance. She was willing to give Neal that chance, and she prayed whatever happened nothing would stop her from doing just that.

All that swimming was draining the boys' energy; Jackson was the first to yawn, and the rest followed.

Neal told the boys; they'd go to bed early that night and be well rested to get an early start in the morning. Jackson asked, "Mom, can I sleep with you and Dad tonight?" Neal looked at Ann to see what she would say. Ann looked back at Neal and her eyes communicated. "This is your call, Dad." Neal knew what was on his mind, but he realized his son had gotten used to falling asleep in his mother's arms. As a newly responsible father, it was going to be his priority to make his son feel safe. Neal laughed and said, "Of course you can sleep with us son." Thomas looked at his mother and father and didn't say a word; his blonde hair was falling into his sky blue eyes. In looks and temperament, he was a combination of Ann and Neal and had the best of both of their features. Thomas stood waiting for the invitation to join them. Jackson had already snuggled down between his parents. He looked at Thomas and yelled, "Get your sleeping bag you can sleep at the bottom of the bed." The next morning when Ann and Neal awoke, their three sons were in their room. A feeling of thanksgiving entered Ann's heart as she whispered a prayer for her family and the chance for a new beginning.

While Ann and the boys were dressing Neal thought about what his parents Robert and Gale told him about how they were disrespectful to his great grandparents, William and Grace Cameron. His great grandparents had tried to share Jesus with his parents after they came home from college promoting humanism. Neal realized this was the same philosophy his parents had raised him with. Neal thought about a professor that had told him that believing in God was archaic. His miraculous healing shattered all of those lies he had been taught. Neal began to thank God in his spirit for bringing him out of darkness. This heresy teaching had been done on purpose to bring the damnable works of men into molding young minds with the theory of humanism rather than the Divine.

Neal felt the tears well up in his eyes. He was thankful he would see his parents again in the new kingdom. How could he have known his parents sharing their story would have an impact on him and his family? His parents revealed that they had become born again Christians. At the time, his brother John and Neal didn't want to hear their conversion story. Their parents had brought them up to believe there was no God. Neal and John had even made jokes that when they were ready to die; they wanted to find God. Neal understood how powerful his parents' prayers were. His parents never stopped praying for him and Ann and the children they would eventually be blessed with. Thankfully, they got to see Benjamin before they died. Benjamin was given a biblical name, so he would be blessed five times over. Their prayers were being answered right before his eyes. His parents had prayed that the blinders would be taken off their eyes and that they would come to know the truth, as it happened with them.

Neal felt sure it was because of his parent's prayers that his suicide had not been successful. Neal thought committing suicide would take the shame off of his wife and sons. He didn't realize that would cause more shame and pain, and allow the spirit of suicide to invade his son's psyche. Addison had been holding Neal's secret of infidelity over his head for almost three years, and he couldn't take it any longer. In Addison sick mind, he thought he had finally found something to bring Ann off her high horse, so Neal kept playing Addison sick games to keep him from destroying his family.

The family vacation had exceeded Neal and Ann's expectations. The boys were in seventh heaven with all they had learned from the guides at the park. They had done everything they set out to do. Jefferson got to take pictures of the bears. Thomas received a trophy for his picture of a Cutthroat trout. Benjamin was able to guide the family on the White Water Rafting Tour; his guide said he was a natural. Sleeping under the stars gave the boys a sense of how vast and beautiful the universe was.

Neal and Ann had reconnected in the past three weeks, communicating with each other in ways they hadn't done in years. Neither mentioned it, but they couldn't believe Addison had not contacted them with some ridiculous story to get Neal back to the office. Neal couldn't believe his family had gone on that many outings in Yellowstone National Park in the three weeks they had been there. He could tell by the look on his sons' faces that they were not ready to return home. Ann could see the reluctance in Neal's face as he told the pilot they would be at the airport by noon. The boys kept crying, "Do we have to go?" Neal and Ann knew they were beginning over again, but they had some unfinished business in South Carolina.

Neal didn't bring up Addison's name while they were on vacation, and Ann made sure not to utter his name from her lips. She was happy to allow Neal's mind to be free and enjoy his sons, in a way they would all remember for a long time.

Chapter Fifteen: Tragedy Strikes

Ann perceived from the tightness in Neal's body and the strain on his face, something was weighing very heavily on his heart, but she was not going to pry. When he was ready he would tell her. Whatever Neal had to say, she knew it would be painful to lose the joy they had the past couple of weeks. The smiles were already being replaced with serious looks, and this made Ann want to run and hide, but instead she prayed for strength.

Ann was allowing Neal to have his own private thoughts. Her days of trying to stay one step ahead of her husband were over; she wanted to remain his wife. If Neal was about to fail, she would be there this time to help him up and not judge. Ann was ready to honor her vows. On their wedding day, Neal repeated these vows to Ann, "To love and to cherish, for better or for worse, for richer or poorer, in sickness and health, as man and wife." Neal reminded Ann they had never said those words to each other. They had made up their own selfish vows that read, "To be equal partners in all things, and keep our faith in ourselves and not in each other." When he thought about those vows, he realized they never married in the sight of God. They did what they wanted, which was to be recognized by the United States, but they weren't sure their marriage was recognized by the sovereign God of the universe.

As the limousine pulled into the driveway of the hotel, they could see the surprised look on the chauffeurs face, when he saw all the luggage that needed to be loaded. He asked the bell captain if he thought the hotel van could carry the rest of the luggage to the airport.

The driver told the boys, "I can see that you young men had a wonderful time." The boys pushed and shoved one another as they climbed into the limousine. Jefferson poked his bottom lip out as if he was two years old. He pushed Thomas and hit Benjamin and said," We don't want to go home." This is our new home." Neal and Ann looked at one another and wished it was that easy to leave everything behind and start over.

Ann took Neal's arm as he helped her into the limousine. They were back to where they started three weeks earlier, headed home, but no one seemed excited to be leaving. The ride to the airport was somber, as if they were traveling to a funeral. Everyone seemed to have a broken heart, but the real heartache was yet to come.

Jake was standing with a big smile on his face as they exited the limo, "Why such sad faces?" he asked. Jefferson said in a childish angry voice, "We don't want to go home." Jake responded, "But don't you miss your friends?" Thomas mumbled, "Our family is the only friends we need." Thomas sounded like he was going to cry any second. Benjamin, trying to be strong said, "Hey guys, stop making mom and dad feel bad. We had a wonderful vacation and we have to go home now. Grow up!"

Ann didn't say a word. She knew the boys would work it out among themselves. After three weeks of laughter and fun, who in their right mind would want to go home?

As they were putting the luggage on the airplane, Ann saw Neal walk to the back of the plane with Jake as if he was giving him instructions. She wondered what that was all about. As they entered the airplane, you could see both men had something on their mind, and it wasn't good.

Neal took Ann's hand as she went to fasten her seat belt, "Not yet Ann," he sighed. Neal took both her hands and looked deeply into her eyes. He began, "Ann, I loved you from the first time I saw you in the board room. I knew you would be my wife. Ann, All I know is that I don't want to lose you. We truly connected these past three weeks; I think you finally saw me as a your husband, and not as someone to be in competition with. I want to thank you for stepping back and allowing me to lead. I know this was new and difficult for you, but it made me feel that you needed me, and I loved having my sons turn to me for help."

"Ann, Addison received my resignation letter this morning through my secretary. I had her hand deliver it to Addison, and not his secretary. I expect to get a call any minute. I asked my secretary to clean out my office and have everything delivered to the house. Ann, there is no need for me to step foot in Addison's firm ever again, when I get back to South Carolina."

Ann almost swallowed her tongue. For a few moments she couldn't speak, and it was a good thing, since Neal had more to say. "Ann please listen with an open heart and mind." Neal's words were like bullets flying from his lips and Ann knew he was going to tell her something that was going deal a fatal blow to her soul. She knew she would need all the faith in the world, because the bullets were about to turn into missiles. In a rush, it came out of his mouth. "Ann, I have asked the pilot to wait till I text him before he takes off; because you may not want to return home with me. After I tell you what's been on my mind. You may want to keep the boys on an extended vacation, since they like it so much here and they have already expressed they don't want to go home."

"Ann, you said you forgive me for everything, but you don't know everything." Neal took a long deep breath and exhaled, "Ann I have twin daughters, and they are two years old." Ann grabbed her chest; she felt as if she was having a heart attack. Neal jumped out of his seat to get her some water. The motion of their father jumping suddenly out of his seat frightened the boys. They turned and saw their mother holding her chest. They ran to her screaming in unison, "Mommy are you alright, mommy what's wrong?" Neal rushed back with the water, and asked the boys to back up to give their mother some air. The boys looked at their father as if to say, "What have you done to mommy?" Neal saw the fear in their eyes, and tried to reassure them "Mommy is okay, I just told her some shocking news." "What news?" The boys asked, "What news?" Neal told the boys to take their seats and he would tell them later, once mommy was feeling better.

Neal had known the news was going to be devastating to Ann, but she had always been so strong and in control, he could never have foreseen her reaction would have been so extreme. He went to cockpit to ask the pilot if he knew if there was a doctor in the airport. The pilot radioed the tower and a doctor entered the cabin within ten minutes. Ann still had not calmed herself by the time the doctor arrived. She was hyperventilating. Neal could see the fear on their son's faces, and their father reassured them that their mother would be okay. The doctor told Neal he should have the pilot take the boys to the hanger and show them some of the planes for a few minutes till Ann calmed down. He told Neal he would give her something to help.

Neal couldn't believe he had been so stupid to have revealed this news to Ann on a plane with no medical help. This was a side of his wife he had never seen. Now it was obvious to him that she was vulnerable like everyone else. After he got the boys to the hanger, he told the pilot he would text him when it was time to bring them back to the plane.

The doctor suggested that they return to the hotel so Ann could rest. He didn't think it was a good idea for her to fly. "Is she going to be alright?" Neal asked the doctor.

The doctor gave Neal a prescription to be filled once they arrived at the hotel pharmacy. The doctor said, "If she needs something to help her sleep tonight, give her only one pill. Have your wife see the hotel doctor in the morning just as a precaution."

Neal walked to the front of the plane with the doctor, looking to be reassured that Ann was going to be okay. The doctor turned to Neal and said, "Whatever you told your wife was a great shock to her system. Her mind is trying to process the information. Mr. Newman, your wife was anticipating that you had some unpleasant news to tell her, and when you went against what she thought you were going to tell her, her mind went into denial."

Neal put his head into Ann's lap and said, "I'm sorry Ann...so sorry." Ann didn't say a word. She just held Neal's head. What could she say? Her husband who told her he didn't want children years before they married. To have three sons with her and now to blindside her by saying he had twin daughters. For three weeks she had thought of all the things that Neal could possibly tell her, and children never entered her mind.

Neal called the hotel to let them know they would be returning. He texted Jake to bring the boys back to the plane. Ann's color had returned to her face by the time the boys walked back in the cabin. They went straight to their mother, "Mommy! Are you okay?" They asked. "What made you sick mommy? Was it the food you ate this morning? Mommy, you scared us." Ann reassured her sons that she was feeling better and she asked them if they would like to stay a few more days at the hotel. They screamed so loud, Neal ran back into the cabin. "What's wrong?" He yelled. "We're going back to the hotel," the boys excitedly announced. Neal was too ashamed and embarrassed to respond because he had caused all of this upheaval.

Ann took Neal's hand, and explained, "Neal, I didn't mean to react the way I did, but you totally caught me off guard. I thought you would have murdered someone, rather than telling me you had more children. There was nothing Neal could say, but "I'm sorry."

Benjamin and Thomas were thrilled to be returning to the hotel, but not Jackson. He was still nervous about his mother's sudden illness. Jackson was no longer interested in seeing the mountains or bears. He was silent in the car with his eyes on his mother.

When they arrived back at the hotel, Neal told his sons to change into their swimming trunks. "We're going swimming. We need to allow your mother to rest for a few hours, doctor's orders." Jackson pouted, "No! I'm not leaving mommy." Jackson was afraid to leave his mother; he'd never seen her so upset before.

Ann said, "Jackson I need to rest, I want you to go with your dad. I'll be fine. Go, you'll have fun playing in the pool with your brothers, and this will give me time to take a well-deserved nap, without you in my bed." Ann laughed. Seeing his mother smile made Jackson feel better. She explained to the boys that she was fatigued from the day's activities in the park. She needed them to give her a couple of hours of rest, and she would be brand new.

Ann could tell from the expressions on her sons' faces, that they weren't buying her act. The boys looked at their father and in unison said, "Dad is this true?" Ann looked at Neal and he read in her eyes not to say anything to the boys. Neal took a deep breath, "Yes boys, your mother needs to rest for a couple of hours." Neal bent down and gave Ann a kiss her on the forehead to reassure her sons everything was okay with their mother. Ann accepted Neal's kiss to assure her sons there was nothing to be concerned about. If she had turned away from Neal at that moment, she knew the boys wouldn't have left the room. Ann could tell her sons intuition told them all wasn't as it seemed.

Ann reached for Neal's arm as he walked away and cautioned "Please don't say anything to our sons about what you told me this afternoon."

Jackson said, "But Mommy, if you get sick again no one will be here to help you, if you need to call for the doctor." Neal was already feeling horrible for causing this uneasiness in his sons. Without a doubt, he clearly hadn't thought his plan through by confessing to his wife when he did. In his mind he saw it going so differently. He knew Ann's first reaction would be anger, then hurt and disappointment in him.

Neal could have never predicted Ann becoming physically ill. No way was he prepared for that reaction. He had considered she might say a few curse words or even have the boys leave the plane or let him have it with both barrels about how disappointed she was, and how he had let his family down. He didn't expect to see her crying and telling him that they would work through the problem or that she forgave him.

Neal was more confused and terrified than ever. No way was he going to be able to tell Ann the rest of his secret. There was only one solution Neal could think of that he found himself in. Neal's solution was Ann was going to ask him for a divorce and full custody of their sons? Neal felt defeated. He wouldn't fight Ann. She could have everything. While Neal stood lost in his thoughts, Ann convinced the boys to go with their father she would be fine, she told them.

Once they left the room, Ann got in the shower and began to sob like a baby. She couldn't believe Neal's betrayal and infidelity had produced children.

Hadn't Neal learned from working for Addison that protection was the first rule of engagement? The executives were taught to always protect themselves from a lawsuit for child support and divorce. Your seed was worth gold, and if you allowed it to get away that seed would reap a harvest for generations to come. It was your family's legacy.

Ann told herself she was ready to forgive Neal for anything he told her, except children out of wedlock, especially girls. The water was calming, and it was bringing clarity to her thoughts. A few nights ago, Neal was fighting in his sleep. She had laid hands on her husband, and prayed that he would be released to confide in her about whatever was tormenting his soul, and that the fear would leave him. He wanted his secret revealed to her, no matter how shocking it might be. She had told herself she was willing to stand by his side. At this moment, in the shower, Ann realized those were words she was saying from her lips and not from her heart.

Neal had broken her heart into a millions pieces and the more she thought about those two innocent little babies thrust into a world of deceit the more she cried. Ann was now crying for two little girls whose names she didn't even know, she couldn't hold any resentment toward these two precious jewels.

Time for Ann had stopped, once she entered the shower. She had no idea of how much time she had spent in the shower. The water was cooling as the tears continued to flow. The water was healing and helping to wash away the pain of a broken heart. She was pretending God was using the water to wash away her evil thoughts of Neal. Truly this was going to be a test to see if she would be able to forgive Neal and if she wanted to continue to be his wife. Ann didn't realize she was sitting on the floor in shower. There were no more tears to shed as she wrapped herself in a towel and stepped out of the shower, into the room. She noticed the clock said 4:30 pm. That meant she had been in the shower for two and half hours.

Chapter Sixteen: Tragedy Strikes Twice

Neal had not returned to the room with the boys; he knew he should keep them away as long as possible. Ann looked in the mirror and saw that her eyes were swollen. Ann needed to find sunglasses, so that the boys didn't see her like this. At that moment, the telephone started ringing, and she looked around the room to see where the sound was coming from. She saw a light flashing on the bed; it was Neal's telephone. He had gone to the pool without taking it. Ann continued to let the telephone ring; she could have cared less about who was calling her husband. The telephone went silent then it started ringing again. This went on for about 20 minutes. Ann thought it might be Addison trying to get in touch with Neal regarding his resignation letter. The telephone wouldn't stop ringing, Ann started to call the pool to have Neal come and get his telephone, but she wasn't ready to see Neal or the boys until she got herself together.

Out of curiosity, Ann picked up Neal's telephone; she had never done this in 15 years of marriage. What did it matter anyway? There was nothing worse than what her husband had already told her. The caller ID said, the State of South Carolina. Ann repeated the words in her head. What reason would they have to be blowing up Neal's telephone? Without thinking, Ann pushed the answer button. A man's voice came on the line and announced "Mr. Newman, my name is Mr. Scott and I'm with the Department of Children and Family Welfare." He had not given Ann time to speak. Ann responded, "No Mr. Scott this is not Mr. Newman. This is his wife, Ann Newman." Mr. Scott asked, "Mrs. Newman, is your husband available?" Ann replied, "No he isn't. Can I help you?" Mr. Scott said, "No Mrs. Newman, it's very important that I speak to your husband; this is a very sensitive and serious matter, and I need to speak with your husband as soon as possible." "Mrs. Newman, I don't know if your husband has informed you about?" Ann calmly said, "Yes, Mr. Scott

194

you must be calling regarding my husband's twin daughters."

Ann could hear Mr. Scott on the other end of the line take a deep breath, as he continued, "Mrs. Newman, I need to speak with your with your husband as soon as possible. It's a very urgent matter that cannot wait. He must contact me within the hour. Here's my number. Thank you Mrs. Newman."

The urgency in Mr. Scott's voice snapped Ann back to reality, obviously something very serious was going on with Neal's daughters, and they needed to contact Neal. Ann pushed her feeling aside for the moment to focus on Neal's daughters. She picked up the hotel telephone, dialed the pool and asked to speak to Neal. Neal answered, "Hello Neal Newman speaking." Ann said, "Neal, a Mr. Scott from Child Welfare from South Carolina called and said it's urgent that you contact him regarding your daughters. Here is the number he left, and Ann hung up the telephone.

Within ten minutes Neal and the boys were busting through the door. "Ann", Neal said in a commanding voice. I know you are not feeling well, and I know the doctor said, you shouldn't fly, but you have to trust me; we have to leave now for South Carolina. I don't want to leave you and the boys here. We all need to be together. Neal turned to the boys and told them to change their clothes and be ready to leave as soon as possible.

Benjamin spoke up, "Dad you're scaring us and Mom's still sick." Ann responded, "No boys, I'm okay. Do as your father said, and get dressed." Ann wasn't okay, but she could hear in Neal's voice that something terrible had happened, and he was almost in tears. Ann finished dressing and found a pair of Louis Vuitton sunglasses to put on. She didn't want the boys commenting on her eyes being red and swollen. They hadn't noticed her eyes, due to all the commotion with their father.

Neal was speechless. He looked pale and unwell. Whatever news he had been given seemed to be worse than what he had revealed to her. From Neal's demeanor, it appeared as if someone had died. She was afraid to ask who.

Ann was shocked by who was standing there to greet them when they arrived at the airport. "Addison?" She thought. Ann wasn't going to get out of the car, but she didn't want to appear childish. Addison's purpose for being at the airport had nothing to do with her, and she'd already had enough excitement for one day. Ann silently said, "God, this is beyond testing." This must be what Elizabeth was trying to prepare her for in her Bible studies. Sometimes the enemy comes in like a flood. Ann had to go into deep prayer for strength and guidance. This was not the time for her to show weakness, especially not in front of Addison. Addison took such a dim view of Christians and believed that all Christian's were weak and their faith was a figment of their imagination.

Neal left Ann and the boys in the car while he talked to Addison. She could see Addison embrace Neal as he buckled to his knees. Ann started to jump out of the car, but the boys beat her to it. They ran and grabbed their dad as he went to the ground. The boys were screaming and crying "Dad are you okay? What's happening?" By the time Ann reached Neal, two men from the hanger, along with Addison, were helping Neal on the plane. The boys tried to assist as well.

Ann was in a daze, and she couldn't believe her eyes. For the first time in 20 years, Ann saw Addison extending compassion to another human being. As Ann got close to her husband, she could see tears streaming down Addison's face, and he was hugging Neal saying everything would be alright. She heard him say, "Neal, whatever you and Ann need, Abigail and I are here." She had never heard Addison use Abigail's name in connection with his.

Addison walked over to Ann and asked how she and they boys were doing. He expressed his sympathy for Neal's misfortune. Addison said, "Ann I know this is a private matter, and I will give Neal the opportunity to explain to you everything that is happening."

Ann was staring Addison in the face. This wasn't the same Addison who had brought destruction and chaos into her life. Addison never asked anyone about their welfare, yet he was asking Ann how she was doing and if there was anything he could do for her. Was this the same person who only a month ago wanted to take Neal off life support? Addison told Ann he had sent for the doctor to give Neal a sedative to calm him.

Addison took a handkerchief from his pocket and wiped his eyes, "Ann, I'm truly sorry for the tragedy that has happened to your family. I need to apologize to you for the role I played in this calamity. I have been wrong for a long time and I didn't realize the suffering I was causing to those around me, because I was so caught up in my own pain. I understand it's going to be difficult for you to find forgiveness in your heart for me, but I pray in the future and in time, you will forgive me. I'm truly sorry for destroying your family. If I had not demanded total loyalty, Neal would never have gotten caught in my web of destruction. I know it's hard to believe that I'm asking for forgiveness, but Ann I'm begging for your forgiveness."

Ann was speechless. She was hearing the words coming from Addison mouth, but what had caused this sudden change? She could see from his body language, Addison was serious concerning the words he was expressing. Ann's was hearing, but her brain was not processing the information.

Neal was stretched out on a small cot being attended to by the same doctor who had cared for her earlier that afternoon. Addison was apologizing to her for his role in whatever was going on with Neal. Her husband was in distress, and she wasn't really sure about why. For a few moments hearing Addison apologize made her forget she was in her own crisis.

Addison told Ann that once the doctor left, he would be returning to Washington D.C., and if they needed him to call. The doctor smiled at Ann as if to say, "This has been a rough day for your family." The doctor told the boys their dad was fine, he had just received some shocking news about a friend, and he was overcome with grief for a few minutes. The boys looked at each other as in disbelief at what the doctor was telling them.

Jackson slid in the seat next to his mother and asked, "Mommy is everything better with you? First it was you and now dad, I'm afraid maybe it will be one of us next." Ann smiled and said, "Jackson everything will be okay," and gently squeezed Jackson to her chest. She leaned closer to Jackson's ear and whispered, "Son in life bad things will happen to good people. There's no way I can't guarantee you they won't happen in your life". Jackson looked at her with a puzzled expression, not quite comprehending what she was saying. Ann laid Jackson's head in her lap as she brushed the hair out of his eyes, and said, "It's alright Jackson don't worry."

After the doctor left, it took about 20 minutes for the sedative to take effect on Neal. Neal stood in the middle of the cabin and apologized to his sons for his earlier behavior. He told them that a dear friend of his had died in a terrible car accident.

Ann let out a loud gasp and grabbed her mouth with both hands. Her heart felt like it was going into her stomach, and her head began to spin. She knew what was happening. And why the Department of Family and Child Welfare had called Neal saying it was urgent that he contact them. She looked at Neal and realized the friend was the mother of his twin daughters, and that she was dead. Ann didn't know her name, but she knew in her gut she was dead. Oh God, she thought what else could happen? She lifted Jackson off of her lap and went to Neal, and he begin to cry on her shoulder. All she could do was think this can't be happening.

Neal's family was standing in the middle of the cabin of the plane holding one another and crying. Ann was crying for his betrayal, Neal was crying out grief, and the boys were crying because their parents were crying. This was like a scene out of a bad movie that seemed to have no ending.

Neal stepped out of the huddle and went to the cockpit to tell the pilot he could take off for South Carolina. Neal's knees were weak, and he didn't know what he was going to do, but he had 95 minutes to come up with a plan that involved Ann. He knew he would have to be respectful of Ann's feeling, but he also knew two little girls would never see their mother again.

When Neal called Mr. Scott earlier, Mr. Scott told him, the girls had been calling for their mommy and daddy since the workers brought them to the office. The children's mother had listed Neal as their father on the paper at the childcare center. The State Highway Patrol contacted the child care center after they couldn't get in touch Neal. The girls were brought to the Child Welfare Department, and he had to pick them up before 10 p.m. or, they would be placed in foster care. If that happened the courts would get involved, and the judge would decide where the children would be placed.

Neal's name was on their birth certificate. That established his paternal relationship to the girls, and all he would have to do is show his driver's licenses and take his daughters home. This was the problem that needed to be solved in 95 minutes. Neal understood Ann wasn't directly involved with his problem, yet as his wife, he knew if Ann told him to take the girls to a hotel he would understand. In no way was Neal giving Ann an ultimatum, but his daughter's needed a place to call home for the night, at the very least.

Neal asked, "The boys if they would like to watch a movie, while he talked with their mother. He took Ann as far away as they could get from the boys. He didn't want to close the curtain, because he wanted to make sure he could see his sons if one of them decided to walk to the rear of the plane. He didn't want them to accidentally overhear their parent's conversation.

Neal said, "Ann, I don't know where to start, if you want me to stay quiet till we land I will, but Ann we have 95 minutes to figure out if you will help me with my daughters and bring them home. Ann, I must be honest and tell you I love my daughters. They're precious to me."

"Their mother's name was Amelia and before her unexpected death today, I had asked her if she would allow us to adopt the girls. I knew that was going to be asking you the impossible. I need to be honest with you. I did care for Amelia. She was a beautiful young woman who was in the wrong place at the wrong time when I entered her life. I want no more deception between us Ann, I had decided to come clean with you before we went on vacation, but I was afraid. I wanted one more chance to see if we could recapture what we had with each other."

"Ann, you gave me hope, when you said, you had been praying for me and you had others praying for us. I heard you, and I had accepted Jesus as my personal

Lord. I wasn't as strong as you, and I wasn't ready to give up the worldly things I had accumulated. I didn't want to give up being in Addison's inner circle. I didn't want to stop seeing my daughters; I wasn't ready to submit until our vacation, and I knew I had to give it all up and walk away."

"Ann, I noticed the change in you immediately and then I remembered the conversations my parents had with me ten years ago. They talked about the love of God and how it changes a person's life. I saw that change in you, but it didn't happen that way for me. That's my confession Ann now it's all in the open."

Ann said, "I have a couple of questions Neal, did Amelia know about me and your sons? You said you cared about her? If you cared for their mother, why would you want to take her children from her?" Neal's face was red from shame as he sighed, "Yes Ann, Amelia knew about you and our sons. She felt very badly and that's why she had intended to abort the babies. I knew I was already wrong for my infidelity, and I couldn't have an abortion on my conscience as well. Ann, I knew you had suspicions that I was unfaithful, and only because of the boys were you were willing to stay in the marriage. I knew you would hate me more if you found out I destroyed two babies lives to cover up my infidelity. That's why I begged Amelia to let us adopt the girls. She wasn't ready to be a mother. Amelia wanted to place the girls for adoption as newborns, but I convinced her to wait, hoping she would fall in love with her girls as you had with our sons."

"Ann, this was one of the reasons why I wanted to commit suicide in order to shield you and our sons from the shame. Addison had been holding this over my head for almost three years, so I couldn't take it any longer. He thought he finally had something to bring you off your high horse, and I had to keep playing his sick games to keep him from using this to destroy our family."

Tears filled Ann's eyes. She could see her father in Neal standing there, and now she understood why the Angel was standing behind her father at the hospital, when he was told he would be a father. The Angel whose language she couldn't understand was trying to tell her he was there to protect her life. Because her father had wanted her aborted, the Angel was telling Ann that as her mother had forgiven her father, she must forgive Neal. It all made sense when her mother said it was time for her to understand.

Ann said, "Neal, you're the head of this family and when I said I have forgiven you, I meant everything imaginable, but I could never have imagined children. It's going to be hard to explain to our sons, that they have two sisters. I'm willing to give these two innocent little girls a chance to have a good life."

Neal, can you believe that Addison asked me to forgive him for his role in all this turmoil? I couldn't believe those words were coming from his mouth." Neal said, "Ann you're not going to believe this, but Addison and Abigail have both given their lives to Jesus. Your friend, Elizabeth, met Sarah, their daughter, and Sarah brought her parents to Elizabeth's home and they both accepted Christ together and got baptized in her pool.

Ann threw her hands up to heaven and said, "Lord this is too much to believe in one day!"

Ann said, "Neal, I haven't even asked, "What are the twins' names?" Neal smiled and said, "Natalie and Natalia."

Chapter Seventeen: Epilogue

Eight years have passed since the vacation where so many lives were forever changed. The twins are ten now, Jackson is 18 and preparing to graduate from high school in June. Benjamin graduated from Harvard law school, and Thomas is in his second year at Harvard. The brothers decided to become defense attorneys.

Neal and Ann started a non-profit for abandoned children. They are also involved in World Ministry for Hurting Children. The Foundation was started and funded by Addison and Abigail Chandler. Their daughter Sarah works with the homeless as youth leader. Joshua, Addison's oldest son became President of Chandler Brokerage firm. Their son, Michael, works with Father Thomas.

There are no true atheists. We are all created in God's image and likeness. Therefore, we can't separate ourselves from the one who created us. No matter how many foster children I love and raise. I did not birth them. Therefore, they were not created in my image and likeness. I can give them the best of me, but my DNA is not in their blood. When God gave us his breath of life, he gave us his very essence.

We have all been born into a fallen world and evil is ever present. Yet, we are not in this world as one without hope. In this life you will have disappointment, betrayal, a broken heart, sickness, disease, suffering and pain, and you will lose loved ones to death.

Addison and Abigail had all the money in the world. Yet they could not find happiness in their soul and peace with one another. Once they found their way together to the source of life, they begin to live a fruitful life. Man can have all the riches of this world, and never find satisfaction for the soul.

Everything in this life is temporary and we must leave it all behind when we exit the stage. The only reason for a person to say the Bible is not true is because he has never studied the written word of God. It's not a fairy tale, but a book that speaks of one man from Genesis to Revelation. He has many names but the name I love best is Jesus. He is the one who changed my life, and he can change yours, if you desire. In this life there will be tragedies and disappointments; it's part of life's journey. In the end all the character's decided to allow God to use them, and to get the glory from their lives. Remember there was only one perfect man. It's not you.

Thank You….

I'm thankful for all 90 members of the **Cameron family**. From the union of two came many. 37 years ago when I came to California, there were only 32 branches from the Cameron tree. Look at how God has blessed.

To my husband **James,** you of all people have seen the best and the worst, but love has been the glue that keeps us together.
To my daughter **Tammey** thank you for being a listening ear.
To my daughter **Stephanie** thank you for all of your editorial tips
To my son **Maurice** thanks for always encouraging me to read.
My sister **Beverly**, sister in law, **Debra**, and my brothers **Rodney** and **Craig** thank you for being my inspiration.
Special thanks to my niece, **Dr. Vanessa Enoch** for final editing and proofreading.
Special thanks to **Barbara S. Byrd** for draft editing.
Special thanks to **Kristal Parks** for finishing her book and lighting a fire under me.

To my children and offspring: **Amadeo, Ashley, Bianca, Erica, Gabriel, Jarod, Jasmine, Jennifer, Jessica, Jocelyn, Joeb, Joshua, Kamea, Karina, Luis, Mauressa, Neirah, Perry Andrez, Samara, Sarai, Zoelle, and Zoey.**